THE PROF

When surgeon Oliver Steele arrives at St Clement's everyone is captivated by his surgical skill and his thoughtfulness for staff and patients alike. Everyone except Sister Sara West, whose encounters with him in her Men's Surgical ward lead her to believe that he's not only Steele by name, but steel by nature, too . . .

THE PROFESSOR'S DAUGHTER

BY
LEONIE CRAIG

MILLS & BOON LIMITED
London · Sydney · Toronto

First published in Great Britain 1984
by Mills & Boon Limited, 15–16 Brook's Mews,
London W1A 1DR

ISBN 0 263 74848 0

Set in 11 on 12½ pt Linotron Times
03–1084–46,000

Photoset by Rowland Phototypesetting Ltd
Bury St Edmunds, Suffolk
Made and printed in Great Britain by
Richard Clay (The Chaucer Press) Ltd
Bungay, Suffolk

CHAPTER ONE

SARA WEST paused to let the warm, August sun waft gently over her upturned face before sighing pleasurably and running up the steps to enter the main block at St Clement's.

'Afternoon, Sister.' The head porter stuck his head out from behind the reception hatch to smile in her direction and proffer a large bouquet of flowers. 'These just came in. They're for one of yours. Mr Dunford, on Men's Surgical.'

Sara smiled and buried her neat little nose in the scent of roses. 'Mm, aren't they beautiful! I love roses. I'll take them up with me.'

Harry watched as the tall, slim, navy-clad figure sped away towards the stairs, then nodded approvingly in the direction of his assistant.

'Best day's work they ever did, promoting that one to Sister. Got a good head on her shoulders. Pretty too. Shouldn't wonder if she's not snapped up in no time. The best ones always are, more's the pity.' Harry sniffed—his life was blighted in winter by a permanent cold and in summer by hay fever.

Totally unaware of his approval, Sara made her way up to Men's Surgical, experiencing the same pleasure now when she entered the bright airiness of the ward as she had two months ago when she had first taken over. It wasn't, she knew, everyone's favourite ward. She had friends who admitted openly that they much preferred Casualty or Outpatients where patients came and went so quickly that there was never any danger of becoming personally involved. The same could hardly be said of Men's Surgical, but in a way, despite the fact that some of the occupants of those beds were very ill, it was that very involvement which Sara loved.

Progressing slowly down the ward now, she smiled, immediately emphasizing what was an attractive rather than a beautiful face, delicate and finely boned. It was her eyes which instantly drew attention. Varying in colour from grey to green according to her mood, the effect was quite startling upon anyone who encountered them, and Male Nurse Jackson was the present lucky recipient as Sara handed him the bouquet.

'These just arrived for Mr Dunford, Nurse. Would you see that he gets them the minute he wakes up.' Her smiling gaze returned from the huddled figure in the corner bed. 'I think you may have to pop over to Grace Ward and beg or borrow a few vases. We're beginning to look rather like a florist's shop.'

Paul Jackson grinned. 'And I expect there'll be a few more when this afternoon's visitors arrive. I'll see to these now, Sister. Oh, and by the way, Dr Lawson rang through about half an hour ago. I explained that it was your morning off and he asked if you'd get in touch whenever convenient.'

'Thank you, I'll do that.' A slight frown marred her face momentarily as she moved towards the small, glass-partitioned office. Tim Lawson was a junior registrar and they were almost, though not quite, engaged. To anyone else it might have seemed an odd arrangement, but somehow a formal understanding had never seemed necessary. One day they would get married. The right time just hadn't arrived yet, partly because she had wanted to continue with her own career, especially after her promotion to sister, and she didn't see how she could do so adequately once she was married to a busy registrar, and partly because . . . well, partly because Tim, being Tim, had never actually got around to buying a ring. She smiled, wondering what he could possibly want. They were supposed to have a date that evening. Perhaps he had to call it off. It was something they were both used to, even though there were times when she accepted it grudgingly.

Seating herself at the desk, she ran her gaze briefly over the messages which were waiting for her and opened the report book to catch up on everything that had happened in her absence. It was important to know precisely what progress (or otherwise) patients had made, whether there had been any new admissions, discharges or changes in treatment. She read intently, warmed by the shaft of sunlight which streamed in through the window and highlighted the auburn tints in her hair, which was coiled neatly beneath the white, frilled cap. The sun emphasised the generous contours of her mouth, which bore the upward curve of both gentleness and compassion.

Her fingers strayed unconsciously to push a strand of hair from her cheek and she looked up as a figure wearing the mauve uniform of a Staff Nurse appeared in the doorway.

'Hi.' Jane Barratt came into the office staring ruefully at her fob-watch. 'Are you early or am I late? Honestly, I don't know where the morning's gone. My feet are killing me.'

'I'm early, just.' Sara gestured her friend to a chair. 'Relax for five minutes. I want you to bring me up to date anyway.' She flipped through the Kardex. 'I don't know what it is about off duties but it seems to take me an age to fight my way back into things.' She frowned. 'Everything looks pretty much the same, except for the emergency admission, Mr . . . ,' she tapped a pen against her teeth.

'Warrington.'

'That's it. Admitted late last night.'

'Suffering from severe chest pain. He was in a pretty bad way and we gather he has a history of heart trouble.'

'Mm. Well, he had a reasonable night. It was obviously a heart attack.' Sara scanned the notes. 'Not a major one, luckily, but he's not going to be out of the woods for a while yet.'

'The registrar saw him this morning and Mr Harrington-Jones is seeing him tomorrow when he does his consultant's round.'

'Well that's fine.'

'Speaking of which, have you heard anything about the new consultant who's taking over from Mr Petrie?'

'Not a great deal.' Sara closed the report book sharply and rose to her feet, going to stand at the glass partition from which she could see the entire length of the ward. 'Arrival is imminent, as they say, and from the little else I have heard, I can't say I'm exactly looking forward to it.'

Jane Barratt looked startled at the rare note of animosity in her friend's voice. 'Why ever not? You don't know him, do you?'

'Lord, no, not personally, but you might say his reputation has gone before him. Apparently Mr Petrie came across him some years ago. In Canada, I think he said, and this man . . . Steele, whatever his name is, was an up-and-coming young thing even then. Making quite a name for himself as a general surgeon.'

'Well, is that a bad thing? I mean, Clem's has a pretty high reputation and it's only natural we attract the best.'

'Oh I'm not against his undoubted qualifications, heaven forbid. I just get the impression he's as keen as mustard and an absolute stickler for efficiency.'

'Well, that's not so unusual, surely? New brooms have a habit of tiring themselves out after the initial burst. I shouldn't think this one is likely to be any different from the rest.'

'Unfortunately I don't think we can count on it. The consultants here at Clem's have always done one full round a week on operating days, as you know. But this man Steele apparently does three, and not just quick visits. I've already been warned it's to be the full thing.'

Jane's eyes widened. 'You're not serious?'

'Perfectly. He'll be taking three operating lists a week and he's already let it be known that he intends doing three rounds complete with medical and nursing students.' She turned from the window, her fingers tapping crossly against the large silver buckle at her waist . . .

'Can you just imagine the chaos that's going to cause, not to mention the time it will take?' Her face flushed faintly with annoyance as she sat at the desk again and pulled the report book towards her. Taking a deep breath, she said, 'I know it's ridiculous, but I've never even met the man and I dislike him intensely already. It's not as if the system hasn't always worked perfectly well the way it is. I don't see that we need any high and mighty newcomer, full of his own importance, to change things.'

Jane gloomily nodded her agreement. 'Still, he may not be so bad when he actually gets here.'

'Well I certainly hope not because I don't fancy working with him and I'd resent having to move. I like Clem's.'

'So do I. Not that I'm likely to run into him as often as you are, being in charge of the ward, of course.'

'I can assure you that if I have anything to do with it, our paths will cross as little as possible.' Sara's lips compressed tightly then her gaze flew to the wall clock. 'Oh damn, I forgot to phone Tim and he left a message for me to specially.'

'Are you seeing him tonight?'

'I'm supposed to be, unless something has cropped up. I thought I might pop home for a couple of hours. I need to collect a few of the things I still have in storage there, and it would be a perfect excuse to see Daddy.'

'How is the professor?'

'Looking distinctly peaky last time I saw him.' Sara's face took on a worried frown. 'I've tried telling him he's overdoing things but you know what they say, doctors always make the worst patients and seldom take any advice except their own, so I'm just wasting my breath when I suggest he slows down.' She sighed, a slight flicker of amusement on her face. 'Anyway, he said something about having a few cronies in for drinks and I more or less promised to put in an appearance if I could. If I ever get finished here, that is.'

Jane accepted the abrupt change of subject and headed for the door. She knew of the very close attachment between the eminent professor of surgery and his daughter, especially since Sara's mother had died a few years ago. She also knew Sara's own unwritten rule that for as long as she worked at St Clement's, she was there strictly on her own merits and not because her father was who he was, and she admired her for the decision that the connection was never mentioned.

'I've got to get back to the ward anyway,' she said. 'We've a new student on. It's her first time on a surgical ward and she's a bit nervy, but I think she'll be fine once she's settled in.'

'I'll see her myself after the visitors have gone.

I'm on 'til eight anyway, which is probably just as well.'

Sara bent her head over the report and was already fully absorbed in it, a slight frown puckering her brow, even before the other girl had closed the door quietly behind her.

The visitors left in dribs and drabs, some eager to get away, others lingering, reluctantly. Sara didn't like to hurry them if their presence didn't interfere with ward routine, but ten minutes after the bell had gone she made a point of walking along the ward and gradually the visitors drifted away, leaving patients to settle to whatever kept them occupied between the tea trolley round and the evening meal which was served at six. Some settled to doze, some read newspapers, others wondered along to the television room. If such a thing existed, it was the quiet part of the day before another rush began when meals were served, medicine rounds were done and staff changed shifts.

The telephone shrilled and Sara reached out automatically to silence it, holding her hand momentarily over the receiver.

'Fine, thank you, Nurse, you may as well pop down to X-ray now. I should think they'll be reasonably quiet, and tell them we'd be grateful if they could let us have Mr Crawford's plates by morning in time for Mr Petrie's round. He's bound to want to see them.'

'Yes, Sister.' Anne Mayford smiled and bustled out of the office, a diminutive figure in the blue gingham of a first year nurse. Sara permitted herself a half smile, then turned to the receiver. 'I'm sorry to keep you. Men's Surgical, Sister West speaking.'

'I should jolly well hope it is.' A male voice chuckled familiarly in her ear. 'I get the distinct impression, Sister West, that you have been avoiding me. Or are you just playing hard to get?'

She frowned abstractedly at the duty list she had been working on and wondered, fleetingly, whether Tim would actually notice if she did play hard to get. 'Oh Tim, I really am sorry. I did get your message and I meant to phone. I just don't seem to have had five minutes. What is it, problems?'

'Well, sort of, but nothing serious!'

'Don't tell me, you can't make it tonight after all.' The tinge of disappointment she felt at the prospect of not being able to see him was only momentary. In this job you soon learned that plans couldn't always be held to. Hospitals demanded something more than a nine-to-five kind of loyalty.

'Oh I can make it. It's just that I'm likely to be a bit late, probably about half an hour, and I thought I'd better warn you so that you're not standing around in the car park. I'm afraid it's been one of those days. The whole list had to be rejuggled because of an emergency. 'We're catching up but you know how it is.'

She did know. 'You sound tired. Are you sure you want to go this evening? I can always make it a flying visit on my own.'

'My dear girl,' he sounded hurt, 'of course I want

to go. You should know by now, I never miss a chance to be with you. In any case it will be nice to see the professor again, if only briefly.'

'Well if you're sure.''

'Perfectly. By the way, I suppose I should also mention that I'm having some slight problems with the car again so if I were you I'd wear something reasonably tatty, just in case . . .'

'Oh, Tim, really.' She gave a sigh of mingled laughter and exasperation. 'When are you going to get rid of that awful old sports car?'

'Get rid?' He sounded scandalized. 'Sweet child, that old car is part of my life.'

She had to laugh. 'I know, but when are you going to get something respectable? More reliable?'

'Probably as soon as I realise my ambition and become a rich consultant, but that's not likely to be for a year or so yet, and in the meantime I'll have to keep tying the old thing together with string and hope it doesn't let me down before then.'

'You're incorrigible,' she said firmly.

'I know, but I love you.'

She heard the teasing laughter in his voice and for once felt too weary to respond. 'Look, Tim, I have to go. I've got an awful lot to get through myself if I'm going to finish on time. I'll see you in the car park at eight-thirty.' She put the phone down quickly, scarcely giving him time to reply, then felt guilty. She was very fond of Tim but there were times when she wondered if he was ever going to grow up, if their relationship was ever going to progress beyond its present stage. She shook her head. It was too late in a busy day to be able to give her brain to those kind of thoughts and her job, and for the moment she was still on duty.

CHAPTER TWO

SHE HAD been waiting by the car for a couple of minutes when Tim's tall, loose-limbed figure came down the steps to meet her. It was still a nice evening, though a breeze had taken the edge off the heat and tugged at her shoulder-length hair which she had purposely left loose. It was always a relief to do away with the restriction of having to wear it coiled beneath a cap all day.

She saw the glance of approval in Tim's brown eyes and her spirits lifted.

'Glad to see you took my advice and dressed sensibly.' He took in the cotton dress she wore. 'We may well end up pushing this heap.'

Her spirits dipped again as she clambered in through the door he opened for her and eased her long legs into the confined space. So much for the time she had spent on achieving that deceptively casual appearance, the careful but discreet make-up, brushing her hair until it shone. The pale lemon dress was new and suited her particularly well, as she had hoped he would notice.

'I suppose you realise I'm going to arrive looking an absolute wreck,' she complained. 'I did tell you Daddy is having guests in. Heavens knows what they'll think.'

He leaned over to kiss her firmly on the mouth

and grinned. 'They'll think you look gorgeous and will be as jealous as hell when they know you're with me.'

In spite of herself she had to laugh. 'I shouldn't think that's at all likely. I doubt if there will be anyone there under the age of about seventy.'

'Well in that case I needn't worry about competition and you can dazzle them with your smile. Honestly, I don't know why you're worrying. You look marvellous, just as you always do. Anyway, I thought it wasn't supposed to be a formal do, just people in for drinks?'

'That's right, it is, but that doesn't mean I have to arrive looking as if I've just . . . pushed a car,' she snapped, tucking a bag containing a dainty pair of high-heeled shoes under the seat. She looked pointedly at her watch. 'Hadn't we better go? We don't want to be too late getting back if we're both on duty first thing tomorrow.'

The car moved slowly through the traffic and in no time they were driving through narrow lanes, heading out into the countryside. It was, Sara thought as she actually felt herself begin to relax, an almost magical process, this change from the noise and bustle and trauma of the town to the peace and quiet she always felt when she went home. It was one reason she had moved out of the Nurses' Home and found herself a small flat, a place she could escape to and retain a little privacy, whilst still being within easy reach of the hospital. But there were still times when she liked to get away altogether, if only for a few hours, like now, and she sometimes found herself wondering what she would do when the time came that her father was no longer there.

She shut the thought off, too disturbed by it to want to carry it through. Although she still missed her mother it was always her father she had felt closest to, probably because it was his love of medicine she had inherited and his encouragement which had finally led to her decision to become a nurse.

She relaxed, sighing, against the seat and it wasn't until they came to a halt and Tim roused her gently that she realised she had actually dozed off.

'Come on, lazy-bones. We made it, and without mishap you'll be pleased to note.'

She struggled into her shoes, flicked a hand quickly through her hair and together they made their way into the house to be met at once by the sound of laughter and voices coming from the sitting room.

'I thought you said just a few old cronies,' Tim muttered, combing his hair and quickly donning a tie which he had whipped out of his pocket. 'It sounds like a party. Do you suppose we should have brought a bottle?'

'Of what?' she giggled. 'Vitamin tonic?'

He caught her to him and kissed her until her cheeks were flushed and her eyes bright. 'Perhaps we shouldn't have come at all. We could always sneak out again. Go somewhere quiet.'

She had to resist the temptation. 'Come on. We'd better at least put in an appearance. It needn't be for long, then I can rush upstairs to collect the box of stuff I want to take back to the flat and we can make our getaway. Daddy won't mind.'

She was aware that she still looked a little dishevelled as they went through into the sitting room. It was a large, rambling old house which had been tastefully furnished over the years with antiques which had been lovingly acquired. The sight of her old home, with its chintz-covered furniture and large fireplaces which in winter would have blazing log fires and which now held huge bowls of flowers, brought a familiar pang of homesickness to her.

The doors were opened on to the terrace and several of the guests had spilled out on to it, carrying their drinks to enjoy the last of the beautiful summer evening. It was there that she saw her father, talking to someone who had his back to them, though even at that distance she found her gaze drawn, briefly, to the tall, powerfully muscular frame of his companion. Obviously her father was not entertaining merely old cronies. That particular one was probably no more than mid-thirties, but there her interest faded as she made her way with Tim across the room to join her father and kiss him lightly on the cheek.

'Sorry we're late,' she said breathlessly, laughing as she found herself clasped in a comfortable, parental embrace.

Her father beamed a welcome which encompassed Tim as well. 'Sara my dear, I didn't think you were going to make it after all. This is marvellous.'

'We very nearly didn't.' She cast a look of amused reproach in Tim's direction. 'It's been one of those days and I'm absolutely gasping for a drink.' She was laughing as she tried to study her father dispassionately, and what she saw sent a shiver of anxiety running through her, though she was careful not to let it show. He looked even thinner than when she had last seen him. His face was drawn and even his hair had lost the last remnants of sandy colouring and was now a shock of grey. She felt a momentary surge of panic well up in her as he held her lovingly at arm's length, smilingly approving her own robust good health. Somehow she managed to contain it—the one thing he hated was fuss and she knew she must control her feelings at least until they were alone.

'Oliver.' He turned now to the man standing beside him. 'This is my daughter, Sara. I was hoping you'd be able to meet her. Not that I ever know for sure when she is going to turn up. You know what a busy life these youngsters lead nowadays.

For the first time Sara felt the full impact of the stranger's dark eyes and her heart thudded as she felt herself scanned by a coldly analytical gaze.

'No, I'm afraid I don't.' He made a slow, ingratiating movement of his head and she felt a shock wave run through her at the arrogance in his eyes. 'Miss West.'

She dragged her fingers away from his grasp, catching the subtle waft of aftershave as he straightened up.

Her father was patting her arm and saying, 'Look, I'll go and help Tim find some drinks. You two get acquainted. I won't be long.' He was gone before she could stop him and she looked around wildly for Tim, suddenly reluctant to be left alone with this man, but Tim was busily engaged in conversation and the look of annoyance was still in her eyes as she turned back to the stranger.

She had had a vague impression of his height when they arrived, yet suddenly even her own five feet six inches seemed dwarfed and she had to look up to meet the chilling gaze which, she realised, had been directed at her steadily ever since they had met.

For a moment she wondered what she could possibly have done to merit the naked look of censure she saw there, then, knowing herself innocent of any crime, she forced herself to meet his gaze directly, her mind vaguely registering the strong, sensual features, the arrogant set of the mouth and jaw and the dark hair which made her wonder whether there might be some foreign blood, Spanish, Italian perhaps, in him?

His voice had held no trace of accent yet she gained the swift and powerful impression that he was a man accustomed to subservience in women, and the knowledge caught her on the raw.

'I take it you work, Miss West?'

The soft drawl of his voice drew her back sharply and she thought she detected a slight note of disapproval which put her instantly on her guard.

She managed a tight-lipped smile, determined,

for her father's sake, to appear friendly. 'But of course. Don't we all? Women do these days, you know. After all, we aren't living in the middle ages.'

The remark had been deliberately provocative and she caught the flicker of sardonic amusement in his eyes.

'You are obviously a believer in women's emancipation, Miss West.'

Was she? She had never seriously thought about it, taking her freedom for granted. In any case it was an argument too deep for her to want to become involved in just then, especially with this man.

'Oh I wouldn't say that exactly,' she flung at him. 'I just happen to believe that there are alternatives to marriage these days for women. That it isn't everything.'

He took a drink from the glass he was holding, studying her above it with a kind of mocking contempt as his gaze drifted to where Tim was standing. 'You don't think so? I'm surprised. I would have thought that any woman would find marriage to the man she loves, fulfilment enough.'

Her eyes sparked angrily. 'Isn't that rather an old fashioned idea, that women should become virtual slaves?' She snapped the words, again not knowing why she did so, except that the idea of being dominated by a man like him suddenly sent a shiver running through her. 'I'm being ridiculous,' she told herself. 'I don't even know him.'

'It's a matter of opinion,' he shrugged lightly, as

if the subject was of little interest. 'Some women may not see it as slavery, but then you are young and perhaps you haven't yet experienced love, Miss West. No doubt you are too busy with other things.'

An angry retort rose in her throat. What right had a perfect stranger to make judgments about her? Then she bit it back, refusing to give him the satisfaction he undoubtedly craved of seeing her rise to the bait. If only Tim or her father would come back . . .

'You're probably right,' she said, sweetly. 'But life is far too short not to make the most of it while one can, don't you think?'

His hand rose, negligently, and she didn't know whether he agreed or not.

'You're not British.' She deliberately made it statement rather than question, and saw his brow lift at the astute judgment. Then she saw the soft tug of amusement at his mouth.

'On the contrary, Miss West. My mother was Italian, my grandfather was Corsican . . .'

'A bandit no doubt,' she thought and lowered her gaze quickly.

'But my father was English and I was born here, which makes me as British as you are.'

Her cheeks tinged with pink as she found herself wondering what wealth of emotions and pagan beliefs he had inherited from such a background. At least it explained the arrogance of his notions about women, she thought, and turned away, gratefully, as her father reached her side and handed her a glass. She took it, sipping at the gin and tonic, glad of anything to occupy her hands.

'Tim has spotted someone he knows so I sent him off for a chat before you leave. I gather you can't stay long.'

'No, sorry. We'd love to but you know how it is.' She kept her gaze purposely averted from the stranger's.

'Well, at least I'm glad to see you two getting on so well.' The Professor beamed. 'Sara is the mainstay of my life, especially since my wife died.'

Feeling the cool stare envelope her, she tucked a hand laughingly through her father's arm and tried to break the tension. 'Don't, darling, you're embarrassing me and I'm sure your . . . guest isn't interested.'

'On the contrary, I am very interested. Miss West.'

She threw him an indignant look and said nothing.

'I shall be sorry to lose her when she eventually decides to marry and settle down.'

Sara felt the colour burn into her cheeks and forced herself to laugh. 'Well, you know that it won't be for some time yet. I intend to see something of life before chaining myself to a kitchen sink.'

'But Tim's a very nice, respectable young man.'

'Yes, of course he is,' she kissed his cheek fondly, 'but I'm not at all sure that that's what I want to settle for. Perhaps I ought to play the field first, to find out.'

Her father chuckled. It was a long-standing joke between them in fact, that she had had few boyfriends, not for lack of choice but simply because all the men she met failed in some way to live up to her expectations. Perhaps she was expecting too much, setting her sights too high, she thought suddenly, but then dismissed the idea. She didn't think so. It was just that, deep down inside her, she had a feeling that she was right to be cautious. Her own parents' marriage had been idyllically happy and she wanted the same, even if it meant waiting until she was really certain.

The shaft of icy disapproval in the stranger's face drove her chin up before she dismissed him peremptorily. After all, her private life was absolutely no concern of his. After tonight they would never meet again.

She caught Tim's arm as he came to her side, full of apologies for having deserted her, and clung to his arm far more intently than she would normally have done.

'Daddy, we're going to have to fly. I really only came to relieve you of some of the stuff I left behind. Now that I have the flat I can use most of it. And I wanted to see how you were.'

'Well, as you can see, I'm fine.'

She accepted the lie, knowing it was what he wished but resolving silently to come again, when they could be assured of privacy. He took her arm. 'Girls these days are so determined to cherish their independence.' He said it without rancour, but again Sara felt the stranger's gaze fixed on her.

'Are you on duty tomorrow?' her father asked Tim.

'I'm afraid so, Sir,' Tim groaned. 'Someone has to keep the old place ticking over.'

'At least until the new Great White Chief arrives, which should be any day now, if he ever deigns to put in an appearance,' said Sara. 'But I for one won't worry if he doesn't, from the little I've heard about him.'

She had turned her back on the stranger and they were half-way to the door when for some reason she flung a glance back over her shoulder, just in time to surprise a look of malevolent humour on the saturnine features before he, in turn, deliberately turned away and began speaking to someone else.

For some unaccountable reason she felt a strange feeling of impending doom run through her before she shrugged it off, laughing.

'I'll try and get down again some time next week, all being well.' She stood on the steps as Tim loaded the box containing her belongings into the car.

Her father kissed her and shook her, gently. 'Take care of yourself my dear. Don't work too hard. You're far too conscientious at times.'

Her smile was crooked as she looked at the tiredness in his eyes. 'I think I must take after you.'

She ran lightly down the steps towards the car and climbed in, conscious, as they pulled away, of the tall figure standing on the terrace watching their departure. She shivered slightly, and Tim looked at her.

'Are you all right? You look a bit pale.'

She blinked and huddled into the cardigan she had brought with her. 'Mm, fine. It must have turned a bit chilly. Either that or someone just walked over my grave.'

She lay her head back against the seat and tried to doze, but for some reason the dark face of a stranger kept intruding upon her thoughts.

CHAPTER THREE

SARA STARED at the silent alarm clock and for one horrifying moment thought she had actually over-slept, until her sleep-drugged senses reminded her that this was her day off. With a sigh of content-ment she huddled back under the covers, allowing herself the luxury of another half-hour's sleep, only to find that when it came to it, habit died too hard to be ignored and her brain was already enjoying a quiet contemplation of how she could spend the off-duty hours.

It had been a fairly hectic couple of days since her visit home. She had managed to find time to phone her father, and as always he had assured her that he was perfectly fit. The feeling of concern she had experienced when she saw him hadn't faded, however, and whilst not arguing, she had resolved to pay that second visit as soon as possible and try to have a serious talk to him.

After that the ward had been thrown into one of its regular chaotic spells but today . . . she rolled on to her back and stretched lazily. Today she could forget all about it and pretend Clem's didn't exist.

It was hot again and a warm breeze drifted in when, five minutes later, she padded through the flat, flinging open windows, and made her way to the bathroom. She was just indulging in a deep, foam-scented soak when the telephone rang and, complaining crossly under her breath, she scrambled out, dragged a towel around her and ran to answer it.

'Hello, Sister West speaking.'

There was a faint chuckle at the other end. 'My, my, we are formal this morning.' Tim's voice almost restored the smile to her face as she realised that she had answered as if she were on the ward. 'And how's my beautiful girl this beautiful morning?'

She stared, frowning, at the damp patch her wet feet had made. 'Actually I was in the bath.'

He made an appreciative sound which brought the colour racing to her cheeks before she said quietly, 'Tim, aren't you supposed to be on duty?'

'Oh, that's all right. I sneaked out for five minutes. No one will miss me.'

She smiled, fighting a feeling of exasperation. 'Honestly, Tim, don't you ever take anything seriously?'

'But of course I do.' There was a faintly injured note in his voice. 'I take *you* very seriously, my sweet.'

Her gaze followed a butterfly as it danced across the garden and she thought of the cooling bath water. 'You know that isn't what I meant. I meant work. Shouldn't you be in theatre?'

'Oh that. Actually we're having a lull. I shan't be needed for hours. Which is why I rang now. Look, it's such a gorgeous day that I thought we might find a pub by the river somewhere later. I'll pick you up at seven if that's okay?'

She wondered with a brief and totally irrational feeling of resentment how he would react if she said she had other plans, or wanted to do something else, then told herself she was being ridiculous. Only minutes ago she had been wondering what to do with herself for the rest of the day, and anyway, a pub by the river sounded perfect. She smiled at the receiver and her own lack of spirit. 'Fine, I'll be ready.'

'See you later then.' He made kissing sounds into the receiver and was gone before she could say anything else.

She returned to the now-cold bath, scrubbed hastily and dressed in her old jeans, telling herself there was absolutely no excuse for not spending some time tidying the small garden which she had been lucky enough to acquire with the flat.

It was midday when the phone rang again. Flushed from the exertion of digging up weeds she dragged the scarf from her hair and tore indoors to answer it. The director of nursing services' voice sounded relieved as she said, 'Oh, Sister, thank heavens I caught you. Look, I'm afraid we have a bit of an emergency and I was wondering if you could possibly help out. I know it's your day off . . .'

Sara brushed that quickly aside. 'That's all right. I hadn't planned anything specific anyway.' Her gaze went to the salad sandwich she had intended having for lunch.

'Oh good.' Miss Baxter's tone lightened considerably. 'The thing is, Sister Andrews has gone off sick. She really shouldn't have come in this morning but she knew we were short staffed with so many people on holiday. Anyway, I'm afraid we've had to send her home, which means we have no one to take charge of Men's Surgical.'

Sara's mind was doing rapid calculations. She glanced at the wall clock and at the grass-stained jeans she was wearing. 'It will probably take me about half an hour, but I'll make it as quickly as possible. If someone can be there to hand over, just so that I have a rough idea of what's happening.'

'Don't worry, Sister. I'll arrange for Staff Nurse Barratt to hang on for an extra half an hour if necessary. I'm sure she won't mind, and I'm very grateful to you.'

She rang off and Sara began a frenzied metamorphosis, shedding the gardening clothes. Soon she stood in front of the mirror in the cool, short-sleeved navy dress with her hair neatly coiled. In winter she would revert to the long-sleeved uniform but at the moment it was decidedly pleasant to feel the sun on her arms as she drove as quickly as the traffic would allow, towards the hospital and parked neatly in the car park. In another hour the visitors would start arriving and she wouldn't have stood a chance of finding a place.

As she hurried to the main doors her gaze rested briefly on a large, sleek black car and she frowned. It was unfamiliar, possibly someone who didn't know the rules, though the spaces were quite clearly

marked 'for the use of senior medical staff only.'
It wasn't a mere status symbol, or perk, as some
people supposed. Surgeons and consultants needed
to be able to get to a patient quickly in an emergency, and wouldn't want to waste valuable time
finding somewhere to park.

She hurried up the steps, taking a renewed
pleasure in the heady scent of the display of roses,
before entering the large swing doors and making
her way lightly up the three flights of stairs to Men's
Surgical where Jane Barratt greeted her arrival
with a wry smile of apology.

'I'm sorry, it's a pity it had to be your day off, but
I'm jolly glad you made it. We've had a bit of a flap
on. Mr Hargreaves went down for his op and it
turned out to be more complicated than they expected, which means, of course, that the whole list
is running late. We also had an emergency admission in about an hour ago. He's down for theatre
this afternoon. By the way, there's talk that the
new man has actually arrived at last, though
I'm not at all sure he isn't a figment of Nurse
Buller's imagination because no one else has seen
him.'

Sara's heart sank as she hurried towards the
office. Jane followed her into the small, glass-
partitioned room, where Sara sat at the desk and
began pulling the report book towards her.

'Oh well, we'll just have to do the best we can.
Can you fill me in briefly on each patient?' She bit
her lip. 'I hate not taking over properly. It's highly
unsatisfactory from everyone's point of view for a

sister not to be fully in the picture about what's going on.'

'Well, you're hardly to blame. You weren't to know that Andrews was going to go off.'

'No, I know. Any idea what was wrong?'

'Bronchitis, from the looks of her. She gets it quite badly from time to time and she was complaining a few days ago of not feeling particularly well.'

Sara sighed. 'If only people would stop trying to be martyrs. Oh, I'm sure she meant well but it causes so much disruption and inconvenience.' She stopped, knowing from her own experience how staff hated to let each other down and that they all tended to be guilty of soldiering on. 'Fire away anyway, and what you can't tell me I'll have to try and play by ear. With a bit of luck I can go through the notes more thoroughly at visiting time and at least we don't have a round this afternoon.'

They sped through the Kardex, a slight frown furrowing Sara's brow as she absorbed the information which her friend gave her as concisely as possible.

'Three patients were discharged yesterday. Mr Grey, Mr Forrester and Mr Thornton, all with Out-patients' appointments except in Mr Grey's case. But the Social Services people have been told. He's likely to need regular visits by the district nurse for some time, at least until he has to be re-admitted, but presumably that will be to Men's Med.'

Sara nodded, battling with a wave of sadness that

for some patients, although they did their best, it was still not enough. 'How about admissions? What about Mr Warrington?'

'He seems to be stable. We're probably going to have a hard time convincing him that he really has to lose weight and cut down if not give up smoking altogether if he wants to avoid another attack.'

'You'd think one would be enough, wouldn't you?' Sara murmured. 'I even had a patient who once told me, quite seriously, that lightning never strikes in the same place twice, and he really believed that once we'd nursed him through a coronary he was never going to have another even though he hadn't the slightest intention of doing anything to reduce the odds. Oh well, you can't win them all, no matter how hard you try.'

The Kardex completed, though not nearly as thoroughly as Sara would have liked, she rose to her feet, looking at her watch. 'Right, off you go now. This is supposed to be your half day and at least one of us might as well make the most of it.'

'I feel horribly guilty.'

'Well don't, for heaven's sake.' Sara laughed. 'As a matter of fact the most interesting item on my agenda was trying to get the garden into some sort of order, so I'm not missing anything. Besides I can take a half day any time when I might appreciate it more.' She grinned. 'Off you go. It's time I made my presence felt anyway.' She ushered the girl out of the office and walked down the ward, pausing to chat at several of the beds as she went.

The lunch trolley had been cleared away, medications handed out and most of the patients were filling the time until afternoon visiting as best they could.

Sara made her way to the bed where a patient due to go to theatre for an emergency appendicectomy was lying with his eyes closed. His face was pale and his eyes seemed to have sunk with pain, although he had relaxed slightly as the pre-med had begun to take effect.

'Hello, Mr Gordon, how are you feeling?' she reached automatically for the board clipped to the end of the bed. His eyelids fluttered open and he managed a faint smile.

'A bit drowsy, Sister.'

'Yes, well don't worry. That's the injection Staff Nurse gave you. It will help you to relax. You'll be going up to theatre shortly and when you wake up again you'll be back on the ward and that pain will have been taken care of.'

'Well, I shan't complain about that, Sister.' He smiled sleepily and she moved on to where a patient was standing at the window looking down on the lawns below.

Standing beside him, she followed his gaze and said, 'Never mind, Mr Lee, you'll be out of here in a couple of days or so, then you'll be able to get in some sunbathing of your own.'

A glint of mischief lit his eyes as he looked down to where a group of nurses were sitting on the grass, relaxing between classes in PTS, and he grimaced ruefully. 'Wouldn't you just know it? Best summer we've had in years and it's just my luck to be stuck in here.'

'I know what you mean,' she laughed. 'But look at it this way. You're better off without that bunion and now you don't have to put off the evil hour any longer. It's over and done with.' She turned, smiling, as a first year nurse came over to her. Nurse Ingram was an attractive girl, her appearance neat, from the pale blue gingham dress to her neatly cut dark hair. She seemed efficient, was polite and did her job pleasantly, and yet Sara still hadn't been able to decide whether Nurse Ingram was really cut out for the job. It was something she wasn't able to put her finger on and it troubled her. Perhaps that was why. Usually she had some kind of instinct which told her at once if a girl was suitable or not, but in this case she could only reserve her judgment and wait.

'Oh, Sister!'

'Yes, Nurse?'

'I'm having a little trouble with bed six. He refuses to take his medication and I wondered if you could perhaps speak to him.'

Sara froze instinctively, her face darkening as she studied the girl. 'We don't treat beds in this hospital, Nurse, we treat patients. Now, what was it you wished to tell me?' She saw the dark flush which rose to colour the girl's face.

'I'm sorry, Sister. Mr . . . Mr . . .'

'You mean Mr Gerard?'

'Yes, Sister.' The girl's expression was one of sullen resentment as it met Sara's. 'Mr Gerard refuses to take his medication and I wondered if you would speak to him.'

Biting back her anger Sara walked across to the patient in question and found the man lying huddled beneath the covers, his eyes closed. She felt an immediate pang of concern at the pallor of his face but hid it as she smiled down at him, automatically reaching to check his pulse. It was thready. As her alarm increased he opened his eyes and she saw the fever brightness of them.

'Hullo, Mr Gerard. Nurse tells me you don't want to take your medication. Aren't you feeling well?'

He opened his eyes to stare at her but said nothing.

'Is the leg giving you any pain?'

He brushed a hand over his eyes. 'It does throb a bit, Sister.'

'Why didn't you tell someone?' she asked gently as she moved to check the traction and eased the covers back to look at the plaster. He had a nasty compound fracture but it had appeared to be healing nicely until now. Her gaze took in the slight puffiness of the toes.

'I did mention it to Nurse, but I know how busy you all are.' His voice faded weakly and Sara's gaze went swiftly, questioningly, to Fiona Ingram. She didn't need to ask if it was true. One look at the girl's guilty face was enough to confirm it.

Her hands clenched with anger as she willed herself not to speak to the girl now. But later . . . Briskly she thrust the chart back at her and forced her voice to a calmness she was far from feeling. Reaching for the thermometer she placed it in the man's mouth. 'I think we'll get someone along to take a look at that plaster, Mr Gerard. It's possible it may be a little tight.' She didn't believe it, unfortunately, but the last thing she wanted was to cause him any anxiety before her suspicions were confirmed.

She was just studying the thermometer reading when a figure moved to stand at her elbow. Assuming it to be one of her staff she didn't turn as she said, 'This is rather high. I think we'll get Dr Lawson along as soon as possible, Nurse, to have a look at Mr Gerard's plaster,' when a voice spoke curtly from behind her.

'There won't be any need for that, Sister. I'll take a look at it myself. What appears to be the trouble?'

Sara stepped back and her mind froze with shock as she looked up into a face which was all too instantly recognisable. She knew that her mouth was open as she struggled to speak, but even before she could do so, the glacial stare had dismissed her and he had taken the chart, officiously, from her hand.

'I take it you are in charge of this ward?'

Feeling slightly sick she forced herself to say, 'Yes, but . . .' Her confused gaze took in his immaculate grey pin-stripe suit, as an awful sense of premonition was beginning to take root in her mind.

'Then kindly be good enough to fill in the details for me, Sister. I don't have all day. I had intended making a round and I'd like to get on with it as soon as possible, if you have no objection?'

She gasped. 'But I have absolutely no idea . . .'

'Surely it doesn't take a personal introduction, Sister. In any case, haven't we already dispensed with that formality, if I remember correctly? In case you've forgotten, however, my name is Steele, Oliver Steele, and I took over from Mr Petrie this morning.'

Her face burned at the contempt she saw in his eyes. So he remembered.

'I made my wishes perfectly clear. I left instructions that I would be taking a round this afternoon. Are you trying to tell me that you aren't prepared?'

She swallowed hard, her mind racing over the information she had tried to absorb in such a hurry. There had been no such message. Or had there? Her heart sank as she remembered the page of notes in Margaret Andrews' large scrawl which she had pushed to one side simply because she hadn't had time to read it. Even so, this didn't justify the attitude of the man facing her now and her chin rose, determinedly as she forced herself to meet the stony gaze.

'I'm very sorry, sir, but I didn't arrive on duty . . .'

'I don't accept excuses, Sister.' He cut her off with a sharpness which stung. 'If the responsibility of this job is too much for you then I suggest you might be better employed elsewhere. I imagine your . . . talents might be suited to something rather less exacting.' The sheer injustice of the words left her white and speechless, but if he even noticed he chose to ignore it as he continued, 'However, right now I have no time to argue. I'd like to get on, if you can spare the time. What seems to be the trouble here?'

She had to force herself to think, to push the fury she was feeling behind her and concentrate on the job in hand. 'I'm rather worried about Mr Gerard. He was admitted suffering from a compound fracture, four . . . five days ago.' She could have bitten out her tongue for the slip which brought a quick, angry glance from the dark eyes.

'Well, which is it, Sister?'

She flinched. 'Four days, Sir.' As if it was her fault that she hadn't happened to be on duty at the time! She beckoned to Male Nurse Jackson. 'Please fetch the notes for this patient as quickly as possible, and then make sure the rest are ready and in order, Nurse. Mr Steele wishes to make a round.' She caught the almost imperceptible raising of Nurse Jackson's eyebrows. 'Quickly, Nurse.' Then she turned her attention to the tall figure bending over the bed, making a very gentle examination of the leg.

It was almost impossible to believe it was the same man when he spoke now, all trace of anger gone as he studied the patient. 'I gather the leg is giving you some pain, Mr Gerard. I'm just going to take a look at it to see what we can do to ease it for you. Do you think you can bear with me for a while? I'll be as quick as possible and try not to hurt you.'

Mr Gerard smiled, thinly. 'You go ahead, doc. I'll hold Sister's hand, if she doesn't mind.'

'Oh I'm quite sure she won't.' Only Sara was aware of the acid note in the words. 'Sister is expert at it. Just you hang on as tightly as you like.'

She clamped her teeth together, hating his arrogance, then deliberately dragged her mind back to the job in hand. After all, she was a nurse and personal feelings shouldn't be allowed to intrude. The fact that Oliver Steele had obviously made his own brief and totally unjust judgment of her was something she couldn't help, but it rankled, especially when she remembered their first meeting and could well imagine why he had drawn those conclusions.

This was hardly the time to do anything about it, however, even if she felt inclined to do so, which she didn't. After all, she didn't owe this man any kind of explanation for what she did in her private life.

Paul Jackson returned with the case notes, which, to her chagrin, Oliver Steele took without as much as a glance in her own direction. He studied them intently for several moments and she found herself becoming aware yet again of the dark hair and the ridiculously long, thick eyelashes which at this moment concealed his gaze.

He looked up decisively. 'I suspect we shall find there's some kind of nasty infection going on under there, Mr Gerard. It's possible there may be some pieces of grit or glass which were too deep for us to see and which are still buried in the leg, working their way slowly to the surface and causing the trouble. The best thing is to get you along to the plaster room as soon as possible. You'll arrange that, Sister. We'll get someone to cut a window in the plaster so that we can see more easily just what's going on and do something about it. In the meantime I'm going to change your antibiotics and give you a booster shot to be going on with. That should knock this infection on the head and we'll have you fighting fit again in no time. How's that?'

It was fine, as far as the patient was concerned. In fact it was galling to Sara to see the ease with which the new senior consultant won over even the most reticent of patients as they progressed along the ward, Sara dutifully, but tight-lipped, a pace behind, determined that he should be given no opportunity for further criticism.

Out of the corner of her eye she saw Nurse Ingram looking miserable and close to tears. 'And well she might,' Sara thought, suppressing the kind of anger which she had thought completely alien to her until now.

'I will see you later, in my office, Nurse,' she managed to say before quickening her steps to follow the tall figure already striding ahead.

The next half hour was an ordeal she wished heartily never to have to live through again, though she immediately recognised the futility of that wish. For better or worse, whether she liked it or not, Oliver Steele was going to be part of her life and every one of her instincts told her that it was very definitely going to be for the worse!

'Can we possibly get a move on, Sister? I haven't got all day. There are other patients needing my attention.'

He stood aside, waiting with an icy calm which Sara suspected was deliberate as she fumbled clumsily for that particular patient's file. Her hand closed on it with a feeling of relief and she couldn't resist a smile of satisfaction as she slapped the folder into his waiting hand. For a moment his gaze mocked her silently before it was lowered over the notes.

'I'd like to see Mr Parfitt's X-rays please, Sister. They don't appear to be here.'

He waited as Sara again turned to the trolley, this time with a dread certainty that she wasn't going to find what she sought. Her voice sounded shrill even to her own ears as it fell into the lengthy silence. 'I . . . I'm afraid we don't appear to have them, Sir.'

He flicked through the notes. 'But they were requested two days ago, urgently.'

'Yes.' Her voice faded, dully, as she remembered she had been on duty when Mr Petrie had sent the patient down to the X-ray department and, knowing that they were rushed off their feet, Sister Andrews had assured her when she took over the ward that she would see they were available for today's round. It was no excuse, however, and Sara knew it. No matter who was to blame, the ultimate responsibility was hers, as sister in charge.

'I'll send Nurse Jackson down for them right away.' She was already beckoning to the male nurse and giving the order as she turned back to

Oliver Steele with a sinking feeling in the pit of her stomach. 'I'm sorry, Sir, I should have . . . would have checked had I known you were going to need them.'

'I would have thought, Sister, that if this ward was efficiently run, it would not have been necessary. How am I to treat patients when half the information I require is missing?'

Resentment brought the colour flooding to her cheeks. 'X-ray has been very busy lately, Sir.'

'I don't consider that sufficient excuse, Sister. I, too, have been very busy. Still am busy, and it doesn't help when this kind of delay happens.' He closed the notes. 'I'll see Mr Parfitt later, when, I trust, the necessary information will be to hand.'

Without giving her time to reply he swung back the curtains and disappeared down the ward leaving her to follow, seething with indignation. The man was utterly, completely unbearable, and if this was a sample of what her working relationship with the new senior consultant was to be like, she didn't think she was going to be able to handle it.

CHAPTER FOUR

SARA had been waiting for the tap at her door, but she steeled herself, taking several deep breaths to calm down before sitting with her hands clasped on the desk and saying quietly, 'Come in.'

Nurse Ingram obeyed, meekly closing the door behind her, and stood in front of the desk. Sara took in the reddened eyes and guessed that the girl had had a good cry in the sluice before obeying the order to present herself in the office, but when she looked for some sign of remorse, it was not there. There was only the sullenness she had witnessed so often and her heart sank.

'You wanted to see me, Sister.' The girl stood with her hands clasped behind her back as her gaze met Sara's, almost insolently.

'Yes, Nurse, and I don't believe I really need to tell you why.'

'No, Sister.'

'Have you any explanation for what happened today?'

The girl dropped her gaze fractionally before it rose again, defiantly. 'I don't think so, Sister.'

Sara checked a feeling of rising anger. 'You do understand the gravity of what you did, Nurse? You do realise why I called you here?' She waited but the girl didn't speak. 'You ignored a patient when he complained to you of feeling unwell.'

'I just didn't think it was serious, Sister.'

'You didn't?' Sara's voice failed. 'You took it upon yourself to make such a judgment?'

'Well, we were so busy. We were rushed off our feet. I simply didn't have time . . .'

'Nurse, we have a ward full of sick people out there. If they were well they wouldn't be here, they wouldn't need us.'

'No, Sister.'

'You have a long way to go yet, Nurse, before you will be in any way competent to judge whether or not a patient genuinely requires help, but in any case, a nurse always makes time, and if a patient complains of feeling unwell, he is never ignored. You could have come to me or Staff.'

'Yes, Sister. I just forgot. I'm sorry.'

Sara's mouth compressed but she tried to force herself to relax. 'I can't help wondering, Nurse, whether you are entirely happy in your work.'

Fiona Ingram's eyes widened. 'Oh but I am, Sister.'

'I've seen very little evidence of it so far. Your attitude towards both patients and senior staff leaves a great deal to be desired and unless it undergoes a radical change, I have to warn you, I don't think you will be allowed to continue.'

The girl's face paled visibly. 'But I do try, Sister.'

'Sometimes, unfortunately, the will to succeed isn't enough. You appear to resent authority and to show a marked dislike for some of the tasks you are called upon to perform.'

'I'm sorry, Sister.'

Sara considered her for a long moment. 'There is no disgrace in admitting that nursing may not be the profession for you after all. If that is the case it's far better to admit it, both to yourself and to us, rather than try to carry on in a situation which clearly makes you unhappy and which, eventually, is bound to affect the standard of care you offer the patient.'

The girl grimaced. 'Well, I will admit, it isn't quite what I expected it to be, Sister.'

'No,' Sara had to smile, 'it rarely is. You'd be surprised how many girls still come to us with the idea that nursing is simply a matter of soothing fevered brows. It is that, partly, but only a very minute part. The other ninety-nine per cent is sheer hard work, much of it not very pleasant, some of it harrowing, hopefully some of it rewarding. But if you don't feel those rewards are worth it . . .' Her hand rose. 'I'm not asking you to come to any decision here and now, Nurse, but go away and think about what I've said. It may be that you would find fulfilment in some other field, possibly even something connected with hospital work but which didn't involve you directly with the wards.' She rose to her feet. 'Anyway, as I said, think it over and in the meantime remember that the patient is our primary concern.' She looked at her watch. 'You'd better get back to the ward now. It's your day off tomorrow isn't it?'

'Yes, Sister.'

'Fine, well use the time to think carefully and

come and talk to me again when you reach a decision.'

She watched as the girl left the office, then sighed. It was always a disappointment when a nurse who had showed initial promise failed to make the grade, and in Fiona Ingram's case she hoped the girl would have the sense to recognise what, to herself, had become increasingly obvious—that she simply wasn't cut out for the work.

She dragged the report book towards her, forcing herself to concentrate as she worked, only to find, to her annoyance, that her attention wandered as her thoughts kept going back to the disastrous afternoon.

Her head ached and without realising it a frown darkened her pretty face. Until now she had always enjoyed her work on Men's Surgical. It was a busy ward which she managed to run smoothly and efficiently, and yet quite suddenly the joy seemed to be going out of it and everything was crashing about her ears. And all because of the arrival of one man.

She toyed with the pen she was holding, stabbing the top on and off until she realised what she was doing and thrust it sharply from her. It was ridiculous the effect Oliver Steele was having on her nerves. She, who had always been so calm, so able to cope. Well, her chin rose, she wasn't going to let Mr High-and-Mighty Steele change that. It was a shame he had had such a bad first impression of her, but she knew she was good at her job and she would jolly well prove it. Not because she cared one jot about his opinion of her, because she didn't, she told herself firmly, but because her own pride demanded it.

Closing the report book she told herself decisively that she wouldn't think about Oliver Steele again. But it was easier said than done. Somehow the incident seemed to have coloured the whole day and she was left with a feeling of depression which hovered as persistently as the headache.

By the time the last patient had returned from theatre she wanted nothing more than to hand over to night staff and crawl back to the flat to lick her wounds and have an early night. It was only then that she remembered she had a date with Tim.

Without giving herself time to think she reached for the phone, and seconds later his voice was talking amiably in her ear. 'Hello my angel, couldn't you bear to wait 'til tonight?'

For once she wasn't in the mood to respond. 'Look Tim, I'm sorry I'll have to cancel. It looks as if I'm going to be late and anyway I'm pretty tired, so if you don't mind, let's give it a miss just this once.'

'Okay, we can go for a drink any time I suppose.'

She heared the vague note of disappointment in his voice and felt a momentary pang of guilt.

'You're sure you're just tired? There's nothing wrong, is there?'

'No, of course not.' She brushed a hand across her eyes. 'It's just been one of those days and I suppose I'm peeved because I'd planned a nice lazy day off and everything seemed to go wrong. Sister

Andrews went off sick with bronchitis, and I had to take over.' She stopped before she found herself getting bogged down with explanations. 'Anyway, I'm stuck until eight and if you don't mind I'd just like to go home and crawl into bed for an early night.'

'Well if you're sure.'

'Yes, quite sure. Sorry.' She put the receiver down and made her way back to the ward just as a white-coated figure came through the swing doors. Her heart almost stopped then her gaze flew to the clock. Surely he wasn't intending to see patients now? Didn't he realise the tea trolley would be arriving at any minute?

If he did, Oliver Steele's expression gave no sign of it as he strode towards her.

'I'd like to see Mr Parfitt now, Sister, if you have no objection. I take it the missing X-rays have been located?'

Ignoring the note of sarcasm she made a frantic signal to Nurse Mayford. 'Yes of course, sir. Bring Mr Parfitt's X-rays from the trolley, Nurse, please, and his notes, quickly.'

She sped away as the tall figure moved towards the bed. Sa·a followed hastily, drawing the curtains, and took the file which Nurse Mayford slapped into her hand with a sympathetic smile before scuttling away.

'The X-rays, sir.'

He took them without as much as a glance in her direction and she waited as he studied the notes for several minutes then held up the X-rays. 'Well, these would seem to verify Mr Petrie's opinion.' He smiled down at the man in the bed. 'That hip joint of yours has been giving you a lot of trouble for a long time and I dare say you'll be pleased to get it seen to so that you can get back to a normal life-style again.'

'You mean you're going to do it?' Mr Parfitt's eyes widened hopefully. 'Tell you the truth, doc, I've almost forgotten what it's like to walk properly and without pain.'

'Yes, I'm sure you have. Well, we're going to change all that. I'm going to give you an artificial joint to replace the old one and in no time at all we'll have you walking around like a youngster again.' He smiled and Sara was treated to an astounding vision of a face which actually seemed quite human. 'Don't worry, Mr Parfitt. I'll put you down for theatre as soon as possible and you'll be out of here before you know it. Won't he, Sister?'

He was looking at her as she managed to murmur something which she hoped sounded reassuring, then the vision faded as he moved to the next bed where a young man whose face was covered in ugly looking bruises met his inquiries with a morose stare.

Sara felt her spirits take a further plunge. Gary Blackford was seventeen, tough and not the easiest of patients because he responded to all administrations with a surly indifference if not outright resistance.

She waited silently as the senior consultant made the usual greetings then flipped through the case notes before bending to take a look at a line of stitches in a head wound.

'Mm, well that's healing nicely. You're not going to make a habit of this sort of fighting are you?'

The young man glared defiantly. 'Yeah, well it helps to pass the time, don't it?'

Sara flinched but Oliver Steele responded perfectly calmly. 'Yes, well I suppose it does, although it seems a somewhat drastic solution to boredom, don't you think?'

Gary sniggered. 'There ain't much choice, mate.'

'You mean you don't have a job?'

'You could say that. Me and thousands of others.'

Sara winced, expecting some show of displeasure, but to her amazement she saw Oliver Steele's mouth twitch very slightly. 'I dread to think what the other fellow looked like.'

'Well he won't be winning any beauty prizes for a while, that's for sure. Going to find himself a bit short of birds too, I shouldn't wonder.'

'Birds . . . oh yes, girls.'

'Right, you got it.' Sara wondered at the sullen expression which had crept back into the boy's face as she waited for the senior consultant to move on. He made no move to do so, however. Quite the contrary. To her astonishment, as she watched, he perched on the edge of the bed, ignoring her frosty gaze at the breach of rules, and seemed to prepare himself for a lengthy chat.

'And how about you? I don't suppose you have any trouble finding girls?'

There was plain fury in Gary's pale face now. 'Are you joking, mate? What bird do you reckon is going to look at me? You know what the kids at school used to call me? Dumbo. It's the ears, get it?'

Sara felt a surge of compassion hit her. It was true, Gary Blackford wasn't the most attractive boy she had ever seen. His ears did protrude quite badly, yet she sensed that all his life he had been subjected to the kind of cruelty of which children were easily capable, and that over the years he had developed a kind of hard shell behind which he could retreat.

'They're really not that bad, you know,' she heard Oliver Steele comment in a remarkably matter-of-fact way.

'Oh yeah, well you should try living with it.' The blue eyes narrowed maliciously. 'But I don't suppose a chap like you has any trouble pullin' the birds, eh? How about Sister there? Bit of all right, yeah?'

She knew it had been deliberate, that he had hit out at anything which would redirect the hurt from himself, but she felt her cheeks flame as the consultant's gaze passed briefly over her. His expression was unreadable as it lingered before he said, calmly, 'I rather think Sister might have ideas of her own about that. Anyway, suppose we did something about those ears while you're in here? We could tuck them back a bit.'

Gary's gaze widened for a moment showing a glimpse of the real uncertainty behind the bravado.

'You're jokin' ain't ya? There's nothing you can do, not really.'

Oliver Steele was busy making some notes on the file he was still holding. 'We'll see. Just leave it to me and perhaps we can do something to improve your love-life as well as your temper, then perhaps we won't see you in here again in too much of a hurry.'

He got up, smiled and said goodbye, leaving Gary Blackford staring after him with an expression of wary hopefulness. Sara said nothing as Oliver Steele moved on without a glance in her direction as if he had completely forgotten her presence. Which no doubt he had, she thought, with irrational annoyance.

At the end of the ward they paused. His white coat was unfastened and she saw the neat, dark pin-stripe suit beneath, caught a faint waft of aftershave as he thrust the case notes at her peremptorily.

How was it, she wondered, that behind those curtains he had actually sounded human, and it hadn't been mere pretence, she was convinced of that. Patients weren't easily fooled, they knew when they were being condescended to, humoured. But there had been no trace of that, merely an awareness of people's pain and problems.

There was no similar understanding, however, in the cool stare he levelled in her own direction now. 'I'll write Mr Parfitt up for some mild sleeping tablets so that he gets some decent sleep before his op. You'll see that he takes them.'

She resented fiercely the implication that she was not to be trusted to perform even so simple a task, and her response was cutting. 'I'll attend to it personally before I go off duty at eight o'clock, sir.'

The sarcasm was lost on him, however, as he said curtly, 'Thank you, I'd appreciate it. The Mr Parfitts of this world soldier on even when they're in pain, and I want him fully rested, not lying awake half the night worrying.'

If he had deliberately tried to make her feel guilty he couldn't have succeeded more and she felt her cheeks colour. 'Don't worry, sir, I'll pop along and have another chat with him before I go off duty and make sure he's all right.'

He nodded briskly, turning away and she walked beside him as far as the office where she was about to leave him when he said abruptly, 'I understand this was to have been your day off and that you came in at short notice when Sister Andrews went off sick?'

Sara couldn't help the look of surprise which widened her eyes as she stared at him. Was he actually trying to apologise for his behaviour earlier?

'Yes, sir, that's right.'

'I see.' Dark eyes assessed her and she was left with the uncomfortable feeling that he was in some way dissatisfied with what he saw as his mouth tightened. 'In that case I believe I owe you an apology for my attitude this morning. I wasn't aware of the facts.'

Nor had he made any attempt to find them out or at the very least given her a chance to explain, she thought, allowing herself an inward smile of satisfaction at his obvious discomfort. Her expression met his levelly. 'That's quite all right, sir. I can assure you that under normal circumstances we would have been fully prepared for your visit, and there will certainly be no similar occurrence in the future, that I promise.'

'I'm glad to hear it. I dislike incompetence, Sister, and whilst I'm prepared to accept that you may not have been aware of my intention to do a round, it doesn't excuse the fact that those X-rays should have been available.'

He was gone, striding down the ward before she had even had time to open her mouth. So much for his apology, she thought, irritably. It proved only one thing, that no matter what she did she was going to be in the wrong as far as the new senior consultant was concerned.

Going into the office she managed to bring her temper sufficiently under control to hand over to night sister. Almost with a hint of devilment she wrote in large letters on the report book: 'Please ensure that all X-ray plates are to hand for Mr Steele's round tomorrow morning, since these are certain to be required.' There was some slight consolation in the thought that it would be her late duty that day, which meant she would miss the event, but there was also the uncomfortable knowledge that she wasn't going to be able to avoid him quite so easily for ever.

CHAPTER FIVE

As it happened, Sara saw nothing of the new senior consultant during the next week. By sheer chance, on the morning when he was due to make his next round she was called to attend a Sisters' meeting, which meant leaving Jane Barratt as senior staff nurse in charge, and by the time she returned there was, thankfully, no sign of Oliver Steele's tall, grey-suited figure.

Jane Barratt furnished the information as she replaced case notes in the filing trolley. 'Oh, he was hardly here any time at all. In fact he really wasn't any trouble.' She gave Sara a sidelong glance. 'Do you suppose we may have misjudged the man? I mean, he seems remarkably human and the patients certainly took to him, especially Mr Cotterill and you know how nervous he is.'

'Typical,' Sara thought, stretching her aching shoulder muscles as she sat at the desk. 'The one occasion I'm not here and he chooses to be civil. I should think you were just lucky to catch him on a good day, more like,' she retorted acidly, and caught her friend's look as Jane perched on the edge of the desk, swinging one neatly clad, black-stockinged leg.

'Oh come on. He is rather dishy, you must admit.'

'Mm.' Sara wasn't prepared to admit any such thing. 'Well it depends if you like the type. Personally I don't. Far too arrogant and full of his own importance.'

'Well, it's all right for you I suppose. You've got Tim, but frankly if he gave me even half an ounce of encouragement I could fall heavily for our Mr Steele,' Jane moaned. 'I rather like the strong silent type myself. Not that there's any chance, worse luck. A man like that must have women flocking after him, falling over themselves to do his bidding.'

'I don't doubt it,' Sara thought drily, refusing to look up from the paper she was reading, though she wasn't really seeing the words at all. 'Anyway, I really don't have either the time or inclination to discuss Oliver Steele's charms or otherwise right now. I have to get this report finished by tonight, and isn't it time the visitors were let in before they break the doors down?'

She knew she had spoken rather sharply and regretted it as Jane left the office with rather a hurt look in her eyes, but somehow the memory of her very first meeting with Oliver Steele and the awareness she had felt then of his sheer masculine virility and undoubted ability to dominate, was suddenly far too vivid and provoked far too many alarming emotions.

For the rest of the day, feeling rather as if she had been granted a stay of execution, she gave herself wholly to her job, seeing patients off to theatre and back to the ward, supervising the drugs and, because they were particularly short staffed due to various nurses being away on holiday, generally helping the junior nurses to lift patients, check drips and, in between times, to attend to the paperwork still requiring her attention.

By the end of the day it was as if every muscle in her body was on fire and she felt almost guiltily relieved that Tim was working too late to expect to see her. There was also the added consolation that she had a half day off in lieu of the one she had missed when she had taken over from Sister Andrews. On a spur of the moment decision she decided to take a long weekend and go and visit her father.

The professor greeted her arrival with the kind of pleasure which both touched her and made her feel guilty that she didn't get to see him more often. Parking the car in the drive she went quickly to where he waited for her at the foot of the steps. She could tell he had been gardening by the comfy old clothes he wore and with which he stubbornly refused to part, despite any amount of coaxing and threats from Mrs Meakin, affectionately known as 'Milly' after fifteen years in what she liked to call the most disorganised, topsy-turvy household she had ever worked in.

He shaded his eyes against the sun then held out his arms. 'Hello, darling, it's lovely to see you again so soon.' He dragged off a pair of tattered gloves and she kissed his cheek trying not to let herself be alarmed by so swift a confirmation of all her previous fears, that he was far from well.

'Where's that young man of yours?'

'Tim? I'm afraid he had to work. Talking of which,' she deliberately changed the subject, 'I see you've been busy too.'

They paused for a minute in companionable silence to look at the large garden with its trees growing in haphazard places and giving a beautiful naturalness to the garden. The lawns had been freshly mowed and the smell of grass and heat mingled tantalisingly to fill her nostrils.

'I've been talking to the roses.' Sir James' eyes twinkled.

'And does it work?'

'Judge for yourself.'

Her gaze caught the brilliant perfection of the blooms and she nodded, smiling, as she slipped an arm through his and they went up the steps to the house together.

'You obviously know just the right words. It's beautiful and it's so nice to be home.'

The professor didn't say anything and she was too deep in thought to catch the quick look he cast in her direction.

Inside the house was cool and airy with windows flung open and bowls of flowers everywhere.

The housekeeper bustled in, her face lighting with pleasure. 'Oh, Miss Sara, it *is* you. How nice! I thought I saw the car. Now just you sit down and I'll bring a pot of tea and some sandwiches. And perhaps now that you're here,' her glance went disapprovingly to Sir James, 'you can persuade someone else to take a rest too.' It was said teasıngly yet Sara caught an undertone even though she managed to respond lightly.

'I'll certainly do my best, Milly, but I've long since realised it's a losing battle.'

'Old fusspot. We'll have that tea outside on the terrace,' the professor muttered, grumpily. '*If there's any chance we'll ever get it, that is.*'

Milly went out, sniffing with the kind of haughty disdain which took no account of social barriers, and Sara hid a smile.

'You're too hard on her. She only worries about you.'

'Well there's no need. I'm perfectly all right and if there's one thing I can't abide it's fussing women. Come on, let me get rid of these.' He tossed aside the gloves. 'Then we can go and soak up the last of the sun while it's still there.'

He sank into a chair and Sara directed her attention purposely away from the lines of tiredness in his face, the tinge of grey about his mouth. 'Are you really, though?' she asked, gently. 'Perfectly all right, I mean? You do look tired.'

'You're not going to lecture me too, I hope.' He sat forward, rummaging in the pocket of his old jacket for a pipe.

'No, not lecture.' Although it was precisely what she would have liked to do. 'But I am worried. I think you need to take things more easily, and the pain is troubling you, isn't it?'

His mouth hardened for an instant, but only an instant before he looked directly at her. 'It's nothing. Nothing for you to worry about anyway.

At my age you have to expect a few aches and pains.'

'I realise that. I am a nurse you know.'

'Yes, well I hope you're not going to go all professional on me. I get enough of that from Dr Sangster—he's like an old woman, forever fussing.'

Sara fought a sudden quickening of her heartbeat. 'You have seen him then?'

'Of course I have.' He knocked his pipe against the wall then began scraping out the bowl. 'How else is he going to earn a living if old neurotics like me don't keep him going?'

'And what did he say?'

'Oh, you know, babbles on about too much smoking, easing up on everything. The man's an idiot. If I gave up any more I'd give up on living.' Suddenly his grey eyes were serious. 'Don't worry about me, Sara. I've no intention of changing my way of life at my age. I'd far rather it went on just the way it has these past seventy years than settle for anything less now. In any case, it would be a bit late, wouldn't it?' He patted her hand. 'Be a good girl, don't fuss.'

She had to swallow hard on all the arguments which immediately rose to her lips. 'All right, I won't. Ah, tea. Shall I pour or will you?'

'May as well make yourself useful now you're here.' The pipe stabbed in the direction of the tray. 'Why *are* you here, by the way? Not just to check up on me I hope, because if so, it's totally unnecessary, as you can see.'

'Not at all,' she handed him a cup. 'I just wanted

to get away, I suppose. It's so quiet and peaceful here.'

'Hm, I thought they were the last things you young people hankered after.'

'Oh it's nice, now and again. Anyway, you know I love coming back here. It's special, always has been.' She drank her tea in silence, trying not to let her fingers tighten on the fragile china.

'It's not like you to run away, Sara.'

Her eyes widened as she stared at him. 'Whatever makes you think I'm running away?'

'I don't. It was purely a guess. But aren't you?'

She stared down at her cup and sighed. 'I don't know. Yes . . . I suppose so. That's the trouble. I'm not sure.'

'The hospital? You still like the work?'

'Oh yes, I love it.' She answered spontaneously then frowned. 'At least I did. I don't know, things have changed somehow. Oh it's not the job. That's what I want to do, and I love Men's Surgical. It's just . . .' Her hand moved in a restless gesture. 'Well I seem to have got off to a bad start with the new senior consultant somehow and I don't know why.' She bit her lip. 'I don't know why it is but every time we meet we seem to strike sparks off each other. He really is the most arrogant, self-opinionated man I've ever met.'

'Funny.' The professor lit his pipe, sending up puffs of smoke. 'He always struck me as being perfectly calm and level-headed. A brilliant surgeon of course. I have the greatest respect for him professionally. Odd, I never found him in the least bit arrogant. Quite the reverse in fact, rather quiet. Doesn't talk too much about his background, although reading between the lines he's had a pretty tough struggle to get where he is. I gather his parents and a sister were all killed in an accident of some kind when he was still very young, and he was brought up by a grandfather.'

'I'm surprised he hasn't married,' she said, with what she hoped was a nonchalant air.

'I believe he almost did. I don't know the details of course, but I gather the lady in question changed her mind and I don't suppose he's eager to repeat the experience.'

Sarah was surprised by the shiver of pity which ran down her spine at the thought of the young boy trying to come to terms with such a tragedy and then a rejection which, she could imagine, would be anathema to a man like Oliver Steele. Perhaps that, together with the kind of unbringing he had had, accounted for his attitude to women, and yet that could hardly be the case, since his antagonism seemed to be directed solely in her own direction. That makes it something rather more personal, she reflected unhappily, helping herself to more tea and trying to thrust thoughts of the new senior consultant out of her mind completely.

Regrettably, the rest of the weekend seemed to fly past and almost before it seemed possible she was loading her small suitcase back into the car and saying her goodbyes. Her father had already gone back into the house to take a telephone call and

Sara took the opportunity to say quickly to Milly, 'If ever you're worried, I mean more worried about Daddy, you won't hesitate to call me, will you? Someone will always get a message to me and I'd come, somehow.' She climbed into the car and wound down the window. 'I know he's more ill than he admits. The trouble is he hates fuss.'

'Then the best thing any of us can do, my dear, is to respect his wishes. Oh I know it's hard and there are times when I scold him, but the alternative to a man like Sir James would be to give up and just die slowly, and your father's not that kind of person. He's always been active, and his brain still is. It's best he enjoys whatever time he has and we help him to do so. It's what he wants.'

Sara nodded bleakly, but as she drove slowly back through the winding lanes, she wasn't at all sure that her reluctance to return to St Clement's stemmed entirely from concern for her father.

CHAPTER SIX

THE WEEKEND away from it all must have done her more good than she realised, Sara thought, as she felt the familiar surge of anticipation the moment she drove through the hospital gates and parked the Mini beneath the trees in the car park.

She had purposely arrived early, despite the fact that she wasn't officially due on the wards until one o'clock, because it gave her time to settle in and take over gradually, rather than having to rush, which left everyone feeling harassed and seemed to set the pace for the rest of the day. Besides which, the unbidden thought came, she had no intention of allowing Mr Oliver Steele to find fault either with herself or the running of her ward again.

Casting an anxious look at the overcast sky she wound up the car windows and felt instantly trapped in the wave of heat which encircled her. Climbing out of the car she was waylaid by a navy-clad figure which came breathlessly to a halt beside her as she bent to lock the doors.

'Phew, I'm melting. I wish it would rain or do something.' Lisa Carson swung a brightly coloured tote bag over her shoulder and collapsed weakly against the car bonnet. 'You'd think I'd shed pounds in this heat, but not a bit of it, and here's you, slim as a rake without the slightest effort. Life can be very unfair.'

Sara smiled at her friend, only too well aware of the constant but losing battle she fought against the inches. 'Never mind, just think of we poor skinnies freezing in the winter when you don't seem to feel the cold at all.'

'Rubbish. I freeze with the rest of you. I just eat more to compensate and this is the result.'

In fact, as Sara well knew, the result was little more than a few pounds which, if anything, merely added to her friend's prettiness and which, if her number of boyfriends was anything to go by, certainly didn't detract from her popularity.

'Are you just going on?'

'Mm, until eight.' Sara dropped the car keys into her bag.

'Poor you. I think I'll just go and find a cool corner where I can collapse into a heap. By the way, I saw Tim Lawson heading this way with a determined look on his face. Ah, talk of the devil. Anyway, I'm off. Don't work too hard.'

'I'll try not to.' Sara waved and was just walking towards the hospital's main doors when Tim's white-coated figure bounded across the grass to her and, with an eagerness which took her slightly by surprise, slipped an arm round her waist and kissed her soundly.

It was some seconds before she was able to detach herself and tuck her neatly coiled hair back into place. 'Well, if this is what going away for the weekend does, perhaps I ought do it more often!'

She glanced at him sideways and frowned. 'Aren't you supposed to be on duty in theatre?'

He grinned. 'It's okay. I got Tony Farrar to cover for me while I nipped out. The next list doesn't actually start for another twenty minutes. Anyway, I missed you.'

'But I was only gone for a couple of days.'

'I know, but it seemed longer, especially as we were extra busy. I'll say one thing, you were right about that new chap Steele. He's a bastard to work for. Seemed to spend the entire weekend trying to put me in my place and finding fault with everything I did.'

The vehemence of his words shocked Sara slightly, even whilst she didn't doubt them for a moment. It merely proved her right. Oliver Steele didn't like seeing his own importance challenged or his authority questioned.

'Oh no, Tim.' She looked at him in dismay. 'What happened?'

He shrugged but she wasn't deceived by the casualness of the gesture. She could tell by his face that he was disturbed by what had happened, and that wasn't like Tim at all. He was always so easygoing. 'Not much. After all, what could he do or say? I was doing my job to the best of my ability, the way I've been taught to do it. It's hardly my fault if he comes along and decides he wants to change things for the sake of making changes and then doesn't like it when everyone doesn't immediately jump.'

They came to a halt in the shade of one of the

large trees which hid them from the sight of the main block.

'What sort of things?' asked Sara.

'Oh, ridiculous things, like insisting on using a specialised instrument he had brought with him when our own trolley was laid up and ready. Our outdated equipment obviously doesn't quite come up to standard.'

There was a faintly sneering tone in his voice which Sara tried to ignore as she frowned, thoughtfully. It wasn't unknown of course for different surgeons to prefer their own instruments. But knowing Oliver Steele he would have made his wishes known in such a way as to put up the backs of everyone in theatre. 'Poor Tim,' she murmured.

'Anyway, the final straw came when he suddenly insisted on fitting another case in at the end of the list. God knows we'd had a hell of a day as it was. Some drunk piled his car into a crowd of shoppers.'

'Was the extra case really so important?'

'It could have waited, as far as I'm concerned,' he said, testily. 'Some kid having his ears flattened. It had waited this long, another few days wouldn't have made much difference, would it?'

Sara bit her lip. 'Was it Gary Blackford by any chance?'

'Mm, I think so. Could have been.'

She nodded, saying nothing, but she couldn't help thinking that to the young man in question it may have made all the difference in the world. However she could understand the kind of tension Tim must have been up against, trying to work in such an atmosphere, and she smiled sympathetically.

'You make me feel guilty, thinking of you working so hard when I enjoyed myself so much.' For a moment she wondered if she had imagined the slightly sheepish look which flickered across Tim's good looking features, then knew she hadn't as he said reluctantly: 'I suppose I'd better tell you myself before someone else does and things get blown out of all proportion. I took Celia Matthews to the pub for a drink, as a matter of fact. That's all it was, just a chance to unwind. Honestly Sara, after what had happened I needed to talk and Celia agreed to come along and listen. It was all perfectly innocent, I promise, even slightly boring if I'm honest. It was a kind of belated celebration too, in a way. She got her Staff a few weeks ago and hadn't had time to do anything special. You know how it is.'

She murmured something, wondering, as a slight tremor of shock ran through her, why he should look so embarrassed if what he said was true and it was all perfectly innocent. 'Of course I believe you,' she heard herself say even while doubts seemed to find alarming chinks in the armour of security she had built around herself. 'In any case you're perfectly entitled to go out with whom you like. After all, it's not as if we are actually engaged, is it?'

She saw the faint colour rush into his face as he turned to face her and pulled her roughly towards him. 'Are you jealous?'

Was she? She needed time to analyse her feelings. 'Not a bit,' she said, briskly. Admittedly it had given her a bit of a jolt to learn that he had taken someone else out, but it was her he was kissing now as she stood docilely in the circle of his arms, her face turned up to his.

It was the voice coming angrily from behind them which made her break from Tim's arms. The colour surged into her cheeks as she turned, to come face to face with Oliver Steele.

'If I may break up this charming little scene,' he said contemptuously, his glance sweeping over Tim (who shuffled uncomfortably) before it came to rest on herself, leaving Sara only too conscious of her dishevelled appearance. 'Is it really necessary to put on such an exhibition quite so close to the hospital where anyone might see, and aren't you supposed to be on duty in any case?' His glance returned to Tim who was now a deathly white. 'I thought you were in theatre this afternoon, Lawson?'

'Yes, Sir, I am but . . .'

'Then I suggest you get along there immediately. I shall be ready to start in ten minutes, with or without you.'

With a tight-lipped glance in her direction, Tim sped away, leaving her to face the senior consultant alone. However he dismissed her with only the merest look of contempt.

'As for you, Sister West, you're running perfectly true to form, I see. I would suggest that you get back to your ward and save your romantic little interludes for a more appropriate time.' And before she could even open her mouth to point out that she was not even officially due on duty yet, he had turned on his heel. She watched the tall, dark-suited figure run lightly up the steps two at a time and disappear through the swing doors before she even realised that she was standing with her mouth open.

She was still fuming when she arrived at Men's Surgical ten minutes later, having taken time to go to the staff cloakroom to dash cold water on her burning cheeks and to fix her white cap firmly on her head. She would show him, she thought, jabbing a white hair-grip viciously into her hair and wincing. Just who did Oliver Steele think he was anyway, interfering in her private life?

Lunches had been cleared away by the time she got on to the ward. The smell lingered sufficiently, however, to make her wrinkle her nose as she beckoned to Male Nurse Jackson. 'Smoked haddock for lunch, I gather. Open the top windows a little, will you? Much as I like fish it does tend to remind you of its presence for a long time afterwards and it isn't very nice, especially for patients coming back from theatre.'

'Right, Sister.'

With a smile on her lips she went into the office where Jane Barratt looked up, mouthing 'hello' as she gave her attention to the telephone she was holding.

'Yes, Mrs Blackford. Yes, he's doing very well. The operation was completely successful as you know, and he seems very pleased with the results.

No . . . yes. He did mention that you weren't able to visit, but certainly I'll give him your love. I expect he'll be home in a couple of days anyway. Yes . . . fine . . . goodbye.' She put the telephone down and rubbed wryly at her ear.

'Gary's mother, I take it?'

'Mm. I think she's feeling guilty because she can't make the journey to the hospital, but I think I've managed to reassure her. I told her he's doing fine. In fact you'd think he was a different person, and not only in looks. The change in him is quite remarkable. All that awful surliness has gone. In fact he's even quite pleasant, helped out with breakfasts this morning and managed a smile with it.'

Sara sat at the desk conscious of the kind of satisfaction she always felt when they had achieved a success. The knowledge that Oliver Steele was responsible for it was something she found herself strangely reluctant to come to terms with, even though she knew she was being churlish. The fact that as a man she found him totally unlikeable, didn't alter the fact that he was undoubtedly a brilliant surgeon and that the patients had absolute faith in him. She had seen evidence enough of that for herself, which made it all the more difficult to understand the antagonism which seemed to have sprung up between the senior consultant and herself.

Sighing heavily she pushed the thoughts away, irritated by the knowledge that, once again, he was intruding upon her life.

'You may as well go to lunch yourself while everything's quiet,' she said as she consulted the rest of the day's theatre list. 'It looks as if we're going to have a fairly easy afternoon. Only Mr Drury to go up, and his op should be pretty straightforward. I can't think why he didn't have those tonsils seen to years ago.'

'Sheer willpower,' Jane grinned, tucking her pen into her apron. 'How was the weekend, by the way?'

'Oh, so so. I tried chatting to Daddy but I may as well have saved my breath. He insists he's fine so that's the way we play it.'

Jane caught the momentary haunted look in her friend's eyes before it vanished behind a facade of briskness.

'Anyway, off you go. You know what the cafeteria will be like in another ten minutes when all the students come rushing out of PTS. You'd think they were prisoners let out on parole.'

'I remember the feeling well, though I have to admit there are times when it all seems a lifetime away. Were we ever that young and innocent, do you suppose?'

'Sometimes I doubt it.' Sara smiled as Jane left the office, then lowered her head over the report. There were times when it was good to remember what things were like before they became complicated . . . before Oliver Steele.

CHAPTER SEVEN

'I SUPPOSE that means the end of summer:' Sara peered disconsolately from her car at the rain lashing over the car park. She felt it matched her mood far too closely for comfort as she got out then ran over to the hospital feeling the water splash icily against the backs of her legs.

The girl hurtling up the steps beside her was more interested in the clock in reception. 'Oh lor, I'll only just make it. See you later, at lunch, if I get any.' Clare Hamilton sped away towards Casualty leaving Sara to discard her dripping coat and gaze ruefully at her mud-splattered tights.

'Damn, now I'll have to change.' She spoke to herself but the head porter, ever on the look-out for a passing conversation, stuck his head out from reception and consulted his watch ominously.

'Have to make it a bit sharpish then, Sister. Orf to a bad start today, are we?'

'You could say that, Harry.' Sara grimaced. 'And I have a feeling it can only get a whole lot worse,' she muttered under her breath as she headed for the nurses' changing rooms. She told herself firmly, as she changed into a new pair of black tights, that it was ridiculous to get so uptight just because it was Oliver Steele's day to do a round.

Luckily, by the time she walked on to the ward, some of her reasoning seemed to have had an effect, and she managed to give at least an outward appearance of calm as she made her way towards the office, pausing to chat to patients as she went. The beginning of the week always saw the intake of routine patients for operations the following day, and she recognised the familiar nervousness, sympathising without actually allowing it to show.

'Good morning, Mr Bennett.' She paused, leaning closer to the occupant of one bed, remembering that staff had warned her that the elderly, military-looking gentleman was hard of hearing. He had been admitted the previous day and was due to go up to theatre in about an hour's time. 'How are you feeling? A little bit apprehensive?'

He nodded affably. 'No good saying I'm not, Sister.' He eyed the breakfast trolley with a certain amusement however. 'Still, just as well it's my turn today. I can't stand scrambled eggs. I suppose it *is* egg?'

Sara craned her neck to peer at the trolley and grinned. 'Now, now, Mr Bennett, it's all good, nourishing food.'

'Oh I don't doubt it, my dear.' Grey eyes twinkled. 'They say an army marches on its stomach. Good thing they don't feed 'em that stuff. Slow 'em up for sure. Shouldn't wonder if it wasn't some sort of enemy secret weapon.' He laughed softly then looked seriously at Sara. 'Be in theatre long, will I? Like to know these things. Life run by the clock more or less, you know. Can't stop the habit.'

She smiled. It was always difficult to be specific in cases when no one knew exactly what would be involved until the operation began.

'I'm honestly not sure. It rather depends . . .'

'Got to wait and see, eh?'

'Yes, well something like that.'

'Ah. Know what you mean. Still, good chaps those doctors.'

'The very best,' she said, firmly. 'You're down for Mr Reece's list and he's a top-class surgeon. But I imagine he's been in to see you.'

'Popped in yesterday afternoon, had a long chat. Put my mind at rest, but you know how it is. Last minute collywobbles.'

Sara held the frail hand in hers. 'Yes, I do know, but try not to worry too much. Staff will be along shortly to give you your pre-med injection. It will make you feel nice and drowsy and help you to relax, and next thing you know, it will all be over and you'll be back on the ward.'

'Problems all sorted out, what?'

Sara smiled. 'I'm sure they will be. Now, would you like a newspaper to read for a while? It might help to take your mind off things.'

She left him avidly studying a crossword and made her way to the office where she read through the night staff report. She then went over the day's routine with members of staff on her ward, allotting specific nurses to the care of specific patients. It made for the kind of continuity she liked and which certainly the patients seemed to prefer. It gave them a chance to get to know a particular nurse and develop a more friendly relationship. It worked both ways, of course, since the nurse was able to gather a much deeper understanding of the individual person's medical needs as well as his personality and background.

Jane Barratt reached for the medicines book. 'We're a bit thin on the ground this morning. Nurse Pickering has a tooth abscess so she's gone to the dentist and isn't likely to be back today, and Nurse Dickson has 'flu.'

'And it would have to be today of all days. Oh well, we'll just have to cope as best we can and hope nothing extra crops up. Will you give Mr Bennett his pre-med. He's a bit fidgety and I don't want him more anxious than he has to be.'

'Fine. Do you want me to go up to theatre with him?'

'Will you? I'll get the case notes sorted out and check that they're all where they're supposed to be.'

The morning routine was set in motion. Breakfasts cleared, medicines given out, beds made and those patients who weren't actually on the list for operations that day, gradually settled to await the consultant's round.

At the thought of that visit Sara's lips automatically tightened and her steps quickened. 'It's high time you'd finished swabbing those lockers, Nurse. Get a move on.' Even to her own ears her voice sounded unreasonably sharp and she made a mental effort to relax, to forget that Oliver Steele was the consultant in question. After all, he's only a man, she kept telling herself as she walked along the ward, her head held high, its neat little cap firmly in place. It was infuriating all the same to feel the pink flush steal up into her cheeks. Why was it, she wondered, that every time their paths crossed, fate seemed determined to give him precisely the wrong impression of her? She bit back a sigh. Well, all she could do was prove him wrong, by showing him for a start that hers was an efficiently run ward and she was good at her job in spite of what he may think of her personally.

The determination settled in her own mind, she gave her attention to the first patients on the list for theatre. Mr Bennett, contentedly drowsy after his pre-med, had been wheeled out of the ward on the trolley by two porters and she made a mental note to watch for his return so that she could be ready with some words of reassurance the moment he began to come round properly. Experience had taught her that patients returning from theatre liked to see a familiar face in that brief moment of waking, even if they didn't always remember after they had slipped into a more natural sleep.

Her gaze went to the clock. Fifteen minutes to the senior consultant's round when Oliver Steele would see each of his own personal patients, those he had already operated on, to check their rate of recovery, and those who would go to theatre either that afternoon or later in the week.

If only she could put the clock forward so that it

would all be over and done with. But she was far too sensible to indulge in wishful thinking. Oliver Steele was a lion to be bearded in his own den.

She felt a twinge of smug satisfaction as her eyes took in the neat rows of beds with their pretty coloured curtains pulled back into place, each locker gleaming fresh with its bowl of fruit or vase of flowers and a jug of water on top. Her gaze travelled to a black plastic sack containing soiled linen and her smile vanished.

'Remove that to the sluice at once, please, Nurse.'

'Yes, Sister.' A little first year nurse scuttled away guiltily with the offending item and Sara felt her mouth twitch, remembering only too well her own nervousness on the wards at the beginning of her training. Things hadn't changed much, she thought, then felt her stomach lurch as the ward doors swung open and, promptly on cue, as the clock hands reached the hour, a dark-suited figure strode briskly towards her.

She drew herself up, hands clasped in front of her. It would give her a great deal of satisfaction to be able to deny him any cause to find fault.

It came almost like a slap in the face to find, however, that far from allowing any of his earlier antagonism to show, Oliver Steele was treating her just like a perfect stranger. Having raked her slim figure, clad in its neat, navy dress, with a single glance which allowed no trace of his feelings to show, he had briskly dismissed her and made his way to the first bed, holding out his hand for the case notes.

'I have a lot to get through today, Sister, so if we can make this as quick as possible.'

The case notes were out of the trolley and in his hands before he could finish speaking. Sara denied herself the luxury of seeing his expression, bending deliberately instead to help the patient unfasten his pyjama jacket and lie back against the pillows.

The tall figure beside her moved to make his examination, his arm brushing briefly against hers in the process, and for some reason the contact was like an electric current passing through her so that she stepped back, quickly, colliding with a young houseman who beamed at her as she stumbled out an apology.

'Think nothing of it,' he whispered as she extricated her feet from his.

A quelling look from Oliver Steele's quick backward glance froze the reply on Sara's lips, and she found the file thrust into her hands as he straightened up.

'May we continue, Sister? If it isn't putting you to too much inconvenience, that is?'

She bit her lip at the sarcasm. 'Not at all, sir.'

'Good. I was saying that I think Mr Vincent will be ready for discharge on Thursday. I'll give him one more going over on my next round but I see no reason why he couldn't go home after that, provided of course that he behaves sensibly and doesn't see it as an excuse to go straight back to work. That isn't the idea at all.'

She watched, curiously fascinated by the smile which briefly transformed the handsome features as he looked down at the man in the bed. 'If I didn't know better,' she said to herself, 'I'd think he was actually almost human.' The notion was shattered as he moved on again, housemen and medical students in tow, and Sara had to dodge smartly ahead in order to whisk the curtains around the next patient's bed and be ready with the case notes before he could ask for them.

There were several very ill patients, one of whom at least would go for operation with little chance of surviving it, and then there were the routine kind of operations which were performed every day and necessitated perhaps only an overnight stay or a few days in hospital. To each, however, Oliver Steele gave the same devoted attention, answering questions as carefully and honestly as possible. It was only when they came to young Gary Blackford's bed that she felt he dropped whatever barrier he had built up for himself. Not that anyone else would be aware of it, of course, certainly not the patients, but she recognised, instinctively perhaps, the need most surgeons had to remain detached from the trauma of caring for the people who placed their lives so trustingly in their hands.

He stood now, relaxed, hands in pockets, and surveyed the young man whose whole attitude as well as appearance had been changed by the recent operation.

'So then, I suppose you'll be wanting to go home

as soon as possible. I don't think there's much more we can do for you here.'

Gary's mouth fell open. 'You mean it?'

'Well, I don't see why not. No reason to keep you sitting around here any longer than necessary, getting in the nurses' way. I imagine you've far better things to be doing.'

'Cor, not 'arf.' Sara didn't miss the wicked gleam in the youngster's eyes as he grinned at the man beside her. 'Got to try out the new style haven't I? I shouldn't wonder if some of my old mates are in for the shock of their lives. What do you reckon, Doc?'

Sara winced at the familiarity but Oliver Steele appeared to find it all highly amusing. 'I think they're going to have to get used to some competition.'

'Too right. So when can I get out of this place then?' He caught Sara's frosty look and grinned. 'Sorry, Sister. It ain't 'arf bad really, but it cramps the style, if you know what I mean?' He winked broadly and she had the distinct feeling that Oliver Steele was enjoying her discomfort immensely, despite the fact that when she looked warningly in his direction, he was busy writing on the case notes and didn't even look up as he said, 'Well, I should think we can turn you loose tomorrow. How's that?'

'Great.' Gary Blackford at least was satisfied with the visit. Sara just longed for it to end as she moved behind the senior consultant and briskly signalled to Jane Barratt to answer the telephone which was ringing with annoying persistence in the office.

As they grouped around the next bed she looked up and through the office window saw Jane mouthing frantically in her direction. She caught the word 'Tim' and saw the telephone receiver raised before some words were exchanged and staff appeared, miming the action of writing something as she glanced towards Sara. It was clearly intended to mean that she had taken a message and left it on the desk.

Sara felt vaguely annoyed. Tim should know better than to ring her when she was on duty, especially when he must know it was consultant's rounds.

Dismissing the matter from her thoughts, she gave her complete attention to the next patient who was not only very ill but also frightened. The curtains were drawn round the bed and Sara donned a gown handed to her by her first year nurse before helping Oliver Steele into a similar garment in order that he could make a special examination.

She almost had to stand on tiptoe to reach the tapes and was ridiculously conscious as she did so of the hair curling at the nape of his neck. Her fingers shook a little then steadied as she directed the waiting nurse to bring in the sterile trolley, her experienced gaze automatically checking that everything which would be required was correctly to hand.

As Oliver Steele scrubbed his hands at the small sink, Sara checked again that the glass tube inserted into a bottle of distilled water was at least five centimetres below the level of the water before turning back to watch as he dried his hands on a sterile towel.

'Let's have the patient propped up, Sister.'

She gestured quickly to the little first year nurse. 'Move those pillows from behind him, Nurse. That's right. Now, can you lean forward, Mr Dakin? Yes, that's fine, rest your arms on this pillow. Nurse, I think we'll need another one. That's it, lean nicely forward.'

She watched, turning her attention again to the man at her side as he said, 'The temperature is still far too high.'

'Yes, Sir, I checked it myself first thing this morning, and he still complains of chest pains.'

'Mm, well obviously we'd better go ahead then and do the pleural drain. It should help matters considerably.'

'The trolley is ready, Sir.'

'Good.' Was there a momentary look of appreciation in his eyes?

'I've already explained the procedure to Mr Dakin since you said it might be necessary to do the drain.'

His brow lifted momentarily as he studied the dark smudge of her eyes. 'Thank you, Sister, I appreciate that. I believe patients have a right to know what is being done to them and why, and in my experience they always react far better. I wish more nurses were conscious of that fact.'

She bent quickly to the trolley, tearing open a

sterile pack containing rubber gloves and watched as he slipped his hands into them. He had very large hands, she couldn't help noticing.

'I always try to instil it into my nurses, Sir,' she said, stiff with embarrassment as she turned to the trolley, checking that the small gallipot was filled with lotion in order that he could clean the area of the patient's skin.

He worked deftly but with the kind of gentleness and skill which she had to admire. Lignocaine was checked then administered, and she arranged the sterile towels, stepping back to watch as he made a small incision in the skin with the scalpel which she slapped firmly into his hand.

All the time Sara spoke reassuringly to the man, trying to ensure that he was caused no more discomfort than was absolutely necessary.

The telephone rang again in the office and Sara frowned, knowing that Jane Barratt had gone up to theatre but, to her relief, out of the corner of her eye she saw Lynda Ray skip towards the office to emerge minutes later and approach her, a frown on her face.

'I'm sorry, Sister,' she whispered. 'That was reception. A patient is on his way in, emergency admission, suspected appendicitis.'

Sara's mind was ticking over frantically, wishing the girl had chosen any moment but this, or that Jane had been on hand to deal with it. 'But we don't have a bed.'

The girl bit her lip as the senior consultant's voice barked out, 'Right, now the trocar.' His hand jerked upwards in an impatient gesture and before she could utter a sound, Sara watched with horror as Student Nurse Ingram, who had been watching the procedure intently, stared with obvious terror at the array of instruments on the trolley and panicked. Before Sara could issue the warning the girl's ungloved hand had closed over the pack containing the necessary item and torn it open, holding it waveringly towards the man whose expression froze.

Immediately Sara leaped to life. 'No, Nurse, no.'

The girl's terrified gaze met hers and Sara saw the tears start up in them at the realisation of what she had done, but this was no time for recrimination or sympathy.

'Go and get a sterile replacement pack, Nurse, quickly, and bring it to me.' She stood, heart thudding, waiting for the explosion of fury which she was sure must come at any moment from Oliver Steele.

Within seconds the pack was placed in her gloved hands and she opened it, handing the trocar to the man beside her. In some ways his silence was far more ominous and she saw the tensing in the nerves of his face as he took it from her.

Sara looked at the white-faced student who was standing at the far side of the bed and, with a nod, gestured that she should leave them. 'Call Lister ward, Nurse, and ask if they can take the emergency admission.'

The girl almost ran down the ward but managed, Sara noted with almost a wry hint of amusement, not to. At least something of her training had been instilled into her. It was a pity her lack of experience had had to show itself right at the vital moment, but it was hardly Fiona Ingram's fault that she had reacted to the surgeon's demand instinctively.

'In fact,' Sara thought miserably, 'I should have anticipated the situation and been ready myself.' Her mouth tightened grimly as the remainder of the treatment proceeded faultlessly. She moved to hold the Spencer Wells forceps whilst he fitted the polythene connection to the tube. There was no sign of the irritation she had seen earlier but she found herself noting the faint lines around his eyes as he concentrated on what he was doing.

With a slight grunt of satisfaction he finally straightened up.

'Right, I think that's it, Sister.'

She felt her own breathing suddenly slow.

'All right, Mr Dakin. We're going to make you more comfortable now and perhaps you can get some sleep. I'll be along to see you again later but I think you'll find that you soon start feeling easier.'

Sara straightened the covers loosely round the patient before supervising the removal of the trolley.

'Coffee, I think, Sister.'

Oliver Steele's words stopped her in her tracks as she stared at him, disbelievingly. Coffee? Surely he must be joking. Hadn't he caused enough disruption on her ward already?

A flicker of amusement—or was it malice?—

crossed his features and she had the unnerving feeling that he had almost read her thoughts.

'If it isn't too much trouble. I missed mine earlier and I have about ten minutes before I start my clinic.'

Her lips tightened on the answer which flew most readily to mind. Anything concerning Oliver Steele meant trouble where she was concerned.

'Of course not, Sir, I'll ask Staff to see to it.' Out of the corner of her eye she caught sight of Jane Barratt's mauve-clad figure returning to the ward. 'I'll have it brought to the office.'

'That's quite all right, Sister, no need for formality,' he said mildly. 'The kitchen will do nicely. This way, isn't it?' He was striding in the direction and Sara snapped her mouth angrily to a close before hurrying after him. Really, just who did he think he was? Unfortunately the question answered itself. He was the Senior Consultant and it was obvious he had every intention of reminding her of the fact.

'I'm sure you would be much more comfortable in my office,' she protested lamely, as he reached to plug in the kettle.

'Nonsense. The kitchen is quite satisfactory. I'm capable of standing up to drink a cup of coffee, you know. If you'll just show me where you keep it.'

She reached into the cupboard, produced the jar and spooned coffee furiously into two cups, adding water as the kettle boiled, and topping up with milk. She pushed the sugar towards him but it was ignored as he stirred his coffee and reached, lazily, for one of the biscuits she set out on a plate. The movement didn't fool her, however. She was firmly convinced there was nothing in the least bit lazy about Oliver Steele. His mind was like a cauldron, despite the apparent outward calm. Her belief was confirmed as he studied her intently and said, 'Relax! I take it even sisters are permitted five minutes for a coffee break? You aren't breaking some hideously ancient rule I know nothing about, are you?'

She flushed, unaware until he spoke that she had been stirring her own cup ruthlessly. The spoon clattered into the saucer. 'No, of course not. As a matter of fact I usually take my break in the coffee lounge. If there's time. Today we just happen to be rather busy.' Her glance stole surreptitiously to her watch and, as always, he was infuriatingly aware of the gesture.

'I'm sorry if my round took rather longer than usual.'

'Oh no.' Her glance flew up, guiltily, but he squashed the protest by saying, 'I'm sorry if it's the case, but I'm afraid it's something you're going to have to get accustomed to.' The unsmiling eyes considered her gravely. 'I believe in talking to my patients, getting to know them as well as their symptoms, and if that means spending time with them, then so be it.'

It was a reprimand and one which was, she thought, undeserved. Or was it? It wasn't the time he had taken so much as the man himself she objected to. And that was ridiculous. Not only ridiculous but highly unprofessional. After all they were both here to do a job, and personalities shouldn't be allowed to come into it. Which meant that it must be some sort of failure on her own part that it happened again and again where Oliver Steele was concerned.

She pushed her cup away and drew herself up. 'An apology really isn't necessary, Sir. On the contrary, if any is to be made then I should be the one to do it.'

His eyes held hers, briefly, and she found herself ridiculously wishing she could interpret the look in them. He said nothing, but then he wasn't likely to make things any easier for her.

She fumbled unnecessarily with the lid of the biscuit tin, refusing to let him see her confusion. 'Obviously I should have impressed the procedure for using the sterile trolley more clearly upon Nurse Ingram.'

'So it would seem.' His gaze was disturbingly cool as he set his cup down, and Sara found herself wishing he would show at least some sign of the irritation he must be feeling and, the galling thing was, that she knew to be justified. There could be no excuse for what had happened, but that didn't lessen her need to try and defend the girl.

'Nurse Ingram is very keen to learn,' she insisted firmly. 'I'm afraid she just panicked. It happened sometimes, even to the best of nurses.'

She heard the gentle sigh escape his lips as he looked at her. 'Does it, Sara? Somehow I can't imagine you making that kind of mistake.'

'Oh, but you're wrong.' Her gaze flew up to meet

his and she felt her cheeks flush. 'After all . . . the ultimate responsibility was mine. I should have foreseen what might happen and prevented it, especially as Nurse Ingram is scarcely out of PTS. I just happen to feel it is important for students to watch and take part in things, that's all.'

He was studying her gravely, his head tilted slightly to one side. He stood with his arms folded, leaning nonchalantly against the table. 'You're going to great pains to defend her, Sara. I wonder why?'

The thought had crossed her own mind too. The incident had only served to confirm her own previous doubts that Fiona Ingram would ever make the grade, but she wasn't ready to admit defeat so easily, especially to Oliver Steele.

'Nurses are human beings,' she declared, stoutly. 'I remember how easy it is to become flustered. All the same, I'm grateful to you for not . . .'

'For not bawling her out, you mean?'

She had the strongest suspicion that his mouth twitched, and certainly the dark eyes held a hint of malicious amusement.

'I don't think it would have helped.'

'I have to agree,' he said calmly, and Sara wondered what it was about his apparent determination to be civil which made it so unnerving.

'I don't see that anything would have been gained by causing a scene and frightening the girl any more than she already was. It doesn't help the student and it certainly doesn't help the patient. In any case,' he added, smoothly, 'I'm sure we both appreciate that Nurse Ingram is not likely to complete the course, don't we, Sara?'

Just for a moment she thought of denying it then sighed heavily, suspecting that he wouldn't be fooled. 'I've been telling myself she just needs time.'

'Unfortunately all the time in the world isn't going to make any difference to some. It's best to accept it. I admire your loyalty, Sara. Unhappily, nursing isn't a profession where we can afford too much trial and error, and in Nurse Ingram's case I think you're just going to have to harden your heart, if that's possible, and let her go.'

Miserably she conceded that he was right, and perhaps it was because she allowed her dejection to show briefly in her face that he suddenly tilted her chin upwards and kissed her, very gently, upon the lips.

It was an incredible experience. Like nothing she had ever known before. The pressure of his mouth had been so fleeting she might almost have imagined it, except for the sudden ridiculous impact it made upon her heartbeat as she stared up at him, blinking in confusion.

'You can't win them all, Sara. Why fight it?'

'Why fight it indeed?' The words echoed in her brain as she fought the sudden breathlessness which seemed to have taken hold of her. Then she swallowed hard to bring herself back to reality as he straightened up quite calmly and moved towards the door, pausing only to say, as if nothing had happened. 'By the way, how is your father?'

The question took her by surprise so that she answered without thinking. 'As a matter of fact I'm rather worried about him.'

'In what way worried?' He was frowning very slightly, watching the nervous gesture of her hand as it pushed back a strand of hair.

'Oh I don't know exactly. Call it intuition more than anything if you like. I just feel that something is wrong. The trouble is, he hates fuss so we never seem to talk about it.' Her voice fell and she hoped he wasn't aware of the slight break in it as emotion threatened to overtake her and she looked at him, blinking back unshed tears. 'Has he . . . has he spoken to you? Do you have any idea just how ill he really is?' She was frowning, unaware that her hands had clenched anxiously together.

For a moment she thought he wasn't going to answer as his brows drew together in what might have been a flicker of annoyance and he studied her for a long moment before he said, 'He's a stubborn man. One I admire very much, and I owe him a great deal.'

His tone was surprisingly gentle and she had to blink hard to get rid of the tears which pricked at her eyes, and which she didn't want him to see. But he was close, very close, suddenly, and with a feeling of panic she had to fight off a crazy urge to throw herself into his arms.

She swallowed nervously, wondering what on earth was wrong with her.

'You're very much like him, Sara.' He was looking down at her in a way which made her heart turn over. 'I hadn't realised quite how much until now.'

It was some seconds before she was aware that the kitchen door was swinging to a close behind him, and even longer before she realised that he had kissed her again, this time slightly more urgently and that, just for a moment, she had responded eagerly to it. And it was that which troubled her most of all as she finally left the kitchen and made her way in a daze back to the office. She closed the door firmly and sat at her desk simply staring at the report book in front of her as she tried to work out just what it all meant.

It was only when she realised she had actually read the page in front of her twice without having taken in a single word that she drew herself up briskly and reached for her pen.

It was ridiculous to allow one simple kiss to affect her in such a way. A kiss which, after all, certainly couldn't have meant anything to a man like Oliver Steele who had gone to no uncertain lengths to let her know exactly what he thought of her. All the same, her hand shook as she pushed back a stray wisp of hair, acknowledging, grudgingly, that, for a few seconds at least, the brief contact had had the most extraordinary effect upon her emotions. She toyed only briefly with a contemplation of what it would be like to be kissed properly by him, held in those arms, and then dismissed it, sighing heavily at the thought that such speculation was not only highly dangerous but also totally irrelevant.

The telephone jangled noisily and she jumped, reaching out to silence it and having to force herself to concentrate as the nursing officer advised her of yet another change of staff.

'I'm afraid it looks as if Nurse Dickson is going to be off for the rest of the week. I'll try to arrange cover from one of the other wards but I can't promise. We seem to be decidedly thin on the ground everywhere at the moment.'

'I expect we'll manage.' Sara heard her own voice sounding reassuringly normal. 'The only time we may run into real difficulty is if we get any emergency admissions or when Staff Nurse Barratt has her day off. But we'll work something out. I don't mind skipping my own off duty this week if necessary.' It seemed to be becoming a habit, she thought.

'Well, I hope it won't come to that. I'll see what I can fix and be in touch again.'

The nursing officer rang off and Sara reached for the duty rosters from the notice-board behind her desk, frowning as she spent the next fifteen minutes poring over them, trying to rearrange duties so that the ward was adequately covered at all times. She scarcely looked up as Jane Barratt tapped and entered the office carrying a Kardex with her.

'This just came up from Admissions,' she announced, putting it on the desk. 'Is it ours or should it go to Lister?'

Sara peered at the form. 'It's Lister's. It's that new admission we had to send over to them because we don't have a spare bed. Heaven knows what we'll do if any more come in. Lister are bulging at the seams as it is.'

'Mm, yes I know. I had Parker bending my ear about it all through coffee. Honestly, you'd think she ran the hospital single-handed.'

'Talking of which, Dickson is apparently going to be off for at least the rest of the week so we're not exactly going to be falling over staff ourselves for a while.'

'Oh lor, that's all we need. Let's hope Pickering gets back, although I should think she's going to be pretty groggy after her visit to the dentist.'

Sara shrugged, dejectedly. 'Well it can't be helped. I've said I'll forego my day off if necessary. I hadn't planned anything specific.' And it would be a relief to be kept busy anyway, the thought intruded.

'I don't mind doing the same if it will help.'

'I was rather hoping you'd say that.'

Jane laughed. 'I'd only arranged a shopping expedition, but a little enforced economising can only do me good. By the way, did you get the message?'

'Message?'

'The one I took while you were otherwise engaged with the great man. From Tim. I left it . . . oh, here.' She reached for the slip of paper tucked under the phone.

Sara took it and read, 'See you tonight.' How typical of Tim to assume that she would fall in readily with any plans he cared to make without consulting her. Her lips tightened. 'I've told him not to ring me when I'm on duty. Sometimes I wonder if he appreciates that I do actually have a job to do. Oh well,' she put the note aside. 'I'll have to catch him later. First I must have words with Nurse Ingram. I've been putting it off but now I'm afraid it can't wait any longer.'

'Oh dear.' Jane grimaced sympathetically. 'Well I don't envy you, but I have to admit I've not been over-happy with her attitude. I heard all about the latest little fiasco when I got back from theatre. I shouldn't imagine it exactly endeared her to our Mr Steele. Not, I would have thought, a man to suffer fools gladly.'

'As a matter of fact he seemed to take it remarkably well.' Sara's cheeks flushed as she remembered that it was she who had received the brunt of his displeasure. 'But it hardly alters the fact that, student or not, Ingram should know better by now than to handle sterile packs.' She sighed heavily. 'I hate to seem hard but I just don't think she's going to make the grade and the sooner she admits it the better it will be for herself and for us. We can't afford to carry passengers in this job.'

Jane eased herself reluctantly from the edge of the desk. 'do you want me to send her in? I haven't seen her around for a while but I rather fancy I saw her heading for the sluice where she's probably having a good cry.'

'Would you? I see no point in postponing the evil hour.' She glanced at her watch. 'Do you want to go to first lunch by the way?'

'Unless you want me to hang on here.'

'No, that's okay. I've enough to keep me busy for a while.' And she didn't relish the possibility of running into Oliver Steele again for a while in any case.

She returned to her work as Jane left the office then, with a sigh, remembered she still hadn't rung Tim. She reached for the phone and his voice, cheerful as ever, answered her own rather stiff greeting.

'Hello, Tim. I only just got your message. About this evening . . .'

'That's all right, my sweet. I'll collect you about eight if that's okay? I'm a bit short of cash so I thought we'd just have shandies or something. You don't mind do you?'

Sara stared at the papers in front of her and found, to her surprise, that she did mind, very much, having her precious free time constantly spoken for and that, for once, she wasn't prepared to submit quite so readily. What she needed more than anything right now was a little time to herself.

'Tim, I'm sorry, do you mind if we give it a miss? I've had a hectic morning and things don't look like getting any better.'

There was an almost imperceptible pause before Tim's drawl, tinged very slightly with annoyance, said, 'What again, sweet? Isn't this becoming something of a habit? Has my boyish charm suddenly begun to fade?'

'Oh come on, Tim.' She heard herself snap the

words whilst supposing, guiltily, that perhaps it was becoming a habit and almost hovered on the brink of relenting, except that for once she genuinely did want an early night. 'I really am sorry, but you of all people know how these things happen and last time I really didn't have any choice but to stand in for Andrews. Unfortunately this time Dickson has gone off sick.'

'I believe you, my sweet, I believe you.' He laughed but even so she sensed a faint note of irritation. 'You don't have to explain. I'm just being selfish in any case. I happen to enjoy your company.'

'And I enjoy yours,' she said, lamely. 'But not tonight, Tim. Perhaps we can make it another time. Tomorrow maybe?'

'No, not tomorrow. As it happens I have to work a late.'

She wondered briefly if the response was almost too quick and whether it was true or whether he had simply decided that she needed a taste of her own medicine. If so, she could only feel surprisingly relieved at the prospect of two free nights and had to keep her voice deliberately bland as she said, 'Oh well, it can't be helped I suppose.' There was a tap at the door. 'Look, I have to go, Tim. I'm about to interview one of my nurses.'

'Fair enough, my sweet.'

'Call me later . . . at home.' She made the pointed reminder and heard the receiver go down almost before she had finished speaking. All thoughts of Tim were put aside however as she called out to the waiting person to enter and Nurse Ingram came in slowly, her face pale and tear-stained as she stood in front of the desk.

'You wanted to see me, Sister.'

Sara almost felt her resolve weaken before the obvious misery in the girl's eyes, but she knew she had to be firm. Too much was at stake in a profession where lives were involved to allow anything other than complete discipline.

'Yes, that's right, Nurse. Sit down.'

Fiona Ingram obeyed, swallowing convulsively as she sat on the edge of the chair, hands knotted nervously in her lap.

Sara studied her for a moment. 'We were going to have a chat, Nurse, after you had had time to think things over.' She smiled gently to give the girl time to compose herself. 'Have you come to any conclusions, any decision?' To her dismay the girl's brown eyes filled with tears.

'Yes, Sister . . . that is . . . I think so.'

'I haven't called you here in order to give out punishment, you do realise that, don't you?'

The girl sniffed hard. 'I know I deserved it, after what happened on the ward. It was . . . it was awful. I can't imagine why I did it. It happened so quickly, instinctively somehow, and yet I knew the moment I touched the packs what I'd done.'

Sara nodded, pitying the girl who had obviously tried so desperately hard. 'Of course I can't say that what happened wasn't important. You have been taught sterile procedures and know the significance of them.'

'Yes, Sister.' She stared down at her hands. 'I just got flustered when Mr Steele asked for the trocar. I just panicked.'

And I can understand why, Sara thought, whilst composing her features.

'If it was just this one incident I would be tempted to say we could overlook it in the hope that it wouldn't be repeated. But I'm not at all sure we could be certain that that would be the case, could we, Nurse?'

Fiona Ingram tugged at the sodden handkerchief in her hand. 'No, Sister, I don't think we could. I do try.' She sighed and dabbed at her nose. 'But somehow it never seems to work out the way I intend.'

'At least we both recognise that there is a problem. Have you come to any conclusion as to what we should do about it?'

There was a momentary silence until the girl seemed to pull herself together and looked directly at Sara. 'Yes, I think so, Sister. I think you were right and the best thing I can do is admit that maybe nursing isn't right for me after all.' She looked away, blinking hard. 'I wish it was. I always dreamed of being a nurse.'

'But somehow it never lived up to those dreams?'

'That's true.' The ghost of a smile flickered briefly. 'I don't know why because I like being with people.'

'Unfortunately sick people don't always respond as we expect them to.'

'That's true. The trouble is that I don't seem to

respond as I expected to either. You saw out there today,' her head gestured towards the ward. 'I went to pieces and it made me realise that I'd be no good at all in an emergency. I just wouldn't be able to cope and I'd let everyone else down.'

Sara scarcely knew what to say. 'Well at least it's something that you have realised that.'

'I thought, at first, it was something I could overcome. But now I know you were right and that perhaps I'd be happier doing something else.'

'Have you any idea what?'

The girl shook her head and Sara caught the trace of tears again. 'It all seems such a waste to give up now.'

'There are times when it takes more courage to do that than to go on. In any case, you've only lost a year and that hasn't been wasted. Far from it. You've learned a great deal which will always stand you in good stead. The important thing is to put it to good use. Have you thought about that yet?'

Again the imperceptible shake of the head. 'No. It's taken time to come to terms with the fact that I'm actually going to have to give up all of this. I'm not even sure that I have come to terms with it really.' This time a tear did make its way down her cheek as Fiona Ingram suddenly lurched to her feet and muttered through clenched teeth, 'I'm sorry, Sister, I really am. I shall give in my notice today. You've been very kind. I only wish I hadn't let you down.'

Before Sara could offer a word of reassurance or dismissal she had fled, leaving her to sit shaking her head and wondering whether she had in some way personally failed the girl.

It was a question she had too much intelligence to pursue. There was no point in taking responsibility for every failed would-be nurse on to her own shoulders. There was always the few who fell by the wayside, yet in a way she would be sorry to lose Fiona Ingram.

Almost reluctantly she made her way on to the ward. It was relatively quiet. The arrival of the lunch trolley was the next major event in the day of patients recovering from ops and finding time hanging heavily on their hands.

She approached one of the beds as its very large, overweight occupant beckoned frantically in her direction.

'Hello, Mr Perkins. Is everything all right?'

Reginald Perkins' eyes watched the advancing trolley eagerly as he hauled himself wheezily up against the pillows. 'I am going to get my curry for dinner tonight, aren't I, Sister?'

Sara managed with difficulty to keep her face straight. 'Is that what you ordered when the lists came round?'

'Oh yes. Very partial to a nice curry I am.'

She wondered fleetingly if there was anything to which Mr Perkins wasn't partial but said, briskly, 'Well if that's what you ordered I'm sure the kitchen will send it up. That's why we ask patients to fill out the menus you see. It helps us to give a little variety and cuts down on wastage too.'

Mr Perkins still looked doubtful. 'I've heard that when you're due for op you get starved for twenty-four hours.'

'Ah,' she hid a smile. 'Well it's not quite that bad but you'd better make the most of it. This will be the last meal you get before your op tomorrow morning, though you'll be given a bedtime drink and if you feel really desperate Nurse will bring you a little water.'

Mr Perkins' doleful expression suggested that the idea held little appeal as he sank back under the covers with a sigh. 'Well I hope in that case they make it a very large curry.'

She left him muttering beneath his breath and contemplating the arrival of the trolley which appeared at that moment through the swing doors. Her nose detected the smell of fish and her stomach contracted as she made a mental note to have salad for her own lunch when she went down to the canteen. As she glanced backward however, she couldn't help noticing that Reg Perkins' eyes had regained their anticipatory gleam as he sat up and dragged the bed table firmly into position, obviously preparing to make the most of his dietary freedom while it lasted.

The windows were open, letting out the lingering wafts of cod and white sauce and the trolley was being wheeled out as Jane came back on to the ward.

'Hi. Your turn. Everything quiet?'

'Blissfully.' Sara nodded through the glass partition of her office to the drowsy figures beyond. 'They're all sated with fish and lumpy potatoes. That should hold them quiet for hours.' She clipped her pen into her pocket and stood up. 'I shouldn't be long. I've decided to settle for a nice, healthy salad.'

'Why not take the chance to put your feet up for half an hour? I can cope here.'

'Mm, I know. But I've promised myself an early night so I'll save myself for that. Thanks all the same.' She headed for the door and stopped, frowning. 'You haven't seen Ingram I suppose?'

'No, why? Oh, of course, the interview! How did it go?'

'Pretty much as I expected, I'm afraid. The poor girl is upset but at least she realises she isn't cut out for nursing. The pity of it is she's nice and she really does want to do something useful.'

'Yes, well unfortunately that isn't always enough, is it? So what's happening?'

'Don't ask me. She fled out of the office in tears saying she was going to hand in her notice. Perhaps I'd better check the sluice as I go past or we'll be under water if she isn't hauled out. Oh dear, why couldn't I have disliked her? It would have made things so much easier. As it is I shall hate myself for weeks.'

'For heaven's sake, why? It's hardly your fault.' Jane grinned. 'Conscience is a hard thing to live with. I was joking. Seriously, there was nothing you could have done.'

'No, well anyway, this won't get me any lunch. I'll love you and leave you. Oh, and just in case he should need reassuring you can tell Mr Perkins if he asks, and I don't doubt he will, that I've checked personally with the kitchen and yes, he'll definitely be getting curry tonight.'

With a wave she left the office and headed through the swing doors, her soft-soled shoes making scarcely any sound as she walked lightly, a smile on her lips, towards the stairs.

At first she thought she had imagined the muffled sound that came from the half-open door of the sluice. She paused fractionally and was about to go on when it came again, except that this time it was quite definitely a sob and with a wave of guilt she realised that she had quite forgotten Nurse Ingram. She moved towards the door, hand outstretched to push it open, only to freeze in her tracks as she heard a voice.

It was undoubtedly a very distressed Fiona Ingram pouring out her misery to some unseen listener. Probably one of the first years, Sara thought, and knew that she should intervene and send them both about their business, cruel as it might seem. There was no place on a busy ward for an hysterical nurse. However, she came to a halt as she heard her own name being mentioned, and was ashamed to find herself blatantly listening.

'I have tried, really I have. But Sister's right. Sometimes wanting something badly just isn't enough, is it?'

There were several convulsive sobs then the answering voice held Sara frozen in her tracks as she heard Oliver Steele say with surprising intensity, 'No, it isn't always enough. But there are different ways of fulfilling a need. Sometimes we choose the wrong one without realising it. In your case it isn't too late to start again. You're still young and you have a great deal to offer, not necessarily on the ward but perhaps in some other aspect of patient care.'

'Do you really think so?' Sara could almost imagine the look of eager hopefulness on Fiona Ingram's face as she said it, and she felt her heart contract painfully at the thought of the man who had somehow managed to inspire it. What an enigma he was, she thought. A strangely contradictory mixture of aloofness and compassion.

It was some seconds before she realised that he was looking directly at her, a frown furrowing his brow as his gaze rose beyond the weeping girl to the neat figure standing now in the doorway.

Just for a second their eyes met and it was as if some barrier had been lowered, only briefly, but long enough for her to glimpse something of the man beyond, and the knowledge left her feeling strangely breathless.

She turned blindly, feeling suddenly like an intruder and imagined she heard him call her name. But she didn't stop to find out. In any case, it wasn't likely. A man like Oliver Steele obviously preserved his more human feelings for the Fiona

Ingrams of this world and Sara had no wish to see the barriers swing up to shut her out yet again.

CHAPTER EIGHT

IT WAS disconcerting to find that her usual ability to sleep well had deserted her completely that night. Despite the kind of all-over weariness which was usual after a long day on the ward, the moment she climbed into bed and closed her eyes her brain seemed to come alive. She was still tossing and turning when she eventually rolled over to look at the alarm and discovered, to her dismay, that it was one in the morning and she was still as wide awake as ever.

Finally, deciding that a warm milk drink might be the answer, she dragged her dressing gown on and padded into the kitchen, putting milk into a saucepan to heat. While she watched it she thought yet again of the incident in the ward kitchen and tried to tell herself that she had imagined the kiss. After all, it had happened so quickly, except that she knew it had been real, just as the emotions it had aroused were real. Far too disturbingly so to be ignored.

None of this made any sense because she didn't even like Oliver Steele. Which, in turn, didn't explain either the sudden heart-thudding curiosity she felt as she wondered what it must be like to be kissed in earnest by him.

It was all pure conjecture of course, she sighed,

pouring the milk on to a generous spoonful of her favourite malted milk drink in a cup and, without switching on the light, carrying it to the window seat in the other room, to sit in semi-darkness, staring out at the garden.

Whether it was the effect of the milky drink or simply lack of sleep finally catching up she couldn't be sure, but a yawn gradually crept up and was stifled before she made her way reluctantly back to bed. Faced with the prospect of being on duty again in a few hours' time and knowing she wouldn't be fit to cope unless she got some sleep, she thumped her pillows and resolutely settled down, closing her eyes. After all, what did one kiss signify anyway? She asked herself wearily. It could have been pity which had prompted it, concern for her father. It could even have been his way of calling some kind of truce between them. It certainly wasn't easy working with the kind of friction which had built up, seemingly out of nothing. But if so, he had certainly used a very unorthodox method of going about it.

Sara yawned and tugged the sheet crossly over her head in an attempt to shut out the image of the tall, autocratic figure. Unfortunately what she couldn't shut out was the persistent memory of his mouth, brushing against hers, a subtle waft of after-shave which had played havoc with her senses, and an even greater awareness that she actually wanted to repeat the experience. But next time she wanted to be ready for it.

Next time, her brain echoed, dully. But there

wasn't likely to be a next time, was there?

She woke late and still tired to a grey morning which became progressively wetter. Arriving at the hospital only to discover that her usual parking space was occupied, she finally managed to find a corner which involved some deft manouevring then a long walk to the main entrance. By the time she entered the swing doors she was not only wet and cross but only just made it to the ward in time and so, it seemed, the pattern was set for the rest of the day.

Luckily the orthopaedic consultant who did his morning round came and went quickly without finding any problems.

'If only they were all like that.' Jane Barratt returned a batch of case notes to the trolley and glanced at her watch. 'Do you want me to go for first lunch?' she asked.

'Would you mind?'

'Not at all. It doesn't really make much difference anyway—I'm on salads. I indulged far too much at the weekend so I'm doing penance.'

Sara smiled and thought that her own appetite probably wasn't going to cope with anything much more solid either, though for very different reasons. She turned her attention firmly to the task in hand, however. 'I'm glad to see Mr Dakin looking so much better this morning. The pleural drain seems to be helping. Has the drainage bottle been changed?'

'Yes, I did it myself.'

Jane clipped her pen firmly into her pocket and

Sara followed her out of the office finding herself wondering, as she went down to lunch three hours later, where the morning had gone.

Luckily the cafeteria was less crowded for the late diners so she was able to find a table, eat her lunch and escape fairly quickly to the staff cloakroom to freshen up before going back to the ward. Her reflection stared back at her from the mirror, hair freshly combed and tucked neatly beneath the white cap, but still revealing its auburn tints. Her features were delicately made up with just a hint of lipstick, yet that did not quite disguise her tension despite a determined effort to relax. Her eyes were shadowed slightly, proclaiming a lack of sleep. Tim always said her eyes were her best feature. Oliver Steele undoubtedly wouldn't agree since they were only too ready to mirror her thoughts and emotions where he was concerned.

She drew herself up sharply, realising with a sense of annoyance that Oliver Steele had managed to intrude into her thoughts yet again without invitation. It was ludicrous, she thought, adjusting the wide belt clasped around her slim waist. Here she was, a perfectly efficient, competent nurse, fully trained, good at her job and yet behaving like a confused adolescent. 'Anyone would think you were in love with the man,' she told her reflection severely, and felt her heart give an odd little leap beneath her starched apron.

'I need a holiday'. The thought flitted temptingly into her mind. She had wondered vaguely about one earlier in the year then her promotion had come along and she had been far too eager to take over her new ward even to think about taking time off. But suddenly she was conscious of feeling tired and less able to cope. Perhaps she could take a few days before winter set in, go away somewhere with Tim, to Wales perhaps. He had relatives over there. She had met them once, a sister and brother-in-law with a boisterous family of three young sons, but Sara had felt instantly at home and had loved the beautiful countryside. She had been equally delighted by the charms of Chester with its lovely mixture of very old buildings and sophisticated shops. Yes, she wouldn't mind escaping for a while and she was sure she could manage to squeeze in a few days' leave. If only Tim could do the same.

It was odd that her thoughts of him should conjure up not Tim himself but Celia Matthews, who came into the cloakroom at that very moment, and whose smile seemed to falter perceptibly as she saw Sara.

She was attractive in a fluffy, blonde sort of way, Sara found herself thinking as she gathered up her things, and the faint flush which was stealing intriguingly into her cheeks at this very moment added to her attraction.

'Hello, it is Sister West, isn't it?'

Sara smiled. 'That's right. And I've seen you on Women's Med, haven't I?'

'Probably.' The girl smiled, self-consciously. 'Though I'm on Casualty at the moment. I got my staff's belt about a month ago.'

'Oh yes of course. Tim told me.'

Celia Matthews' eyes widened fractionally 'T . . . Dr Lawson told you?'

'Yes, I think so. I'm sure he mentioned in passing that you'd shared a celebratory drink. Something like that.'

The girl laughed awkwardly. 'Oh well, as long as you don't mind.'

'Mind? No, of course not.' Sara wondered why her own smile was suddenly stiff and unreal. 'Why should I? After all Dr Lawson is a perfectly free agent.'

All the same, without quite knowing why, she couldn't shake off the slight feeling of depression which accompanied her back to the ward as she remembered the very definite look of relief which had flashed just for a second into the girl's eyes.

There was no time to dwell on it, however, as the day progressed relentlessly on. In any case it probably meant nothing at all. She may even have imagined it. Either way she was seeing Tim tonight, a routine which smacked sufficiently of normality to allow her to put it to the back of her mind for the present at least.

It was six-thirty before she finally handed over the ward and went off duty, which just gave her time for a relaxing soak in a hot bath before getting changed into a soft, woollen dress which though comfortable didn't exactly add to her attractions. Not that they were much in evidence at the moment anyway, she decided, as she sat in front of the mirror to apply a thin covering of make-up and flick a comb through her hair. But it was hard to raise any enthusiasm even for a drink at the pub with Tim after a long, tiring day.

She sighed, telling herself that she wasn't being fair. One of these days she was going to have to come to a decision about herself and Tim and their future together, if there was to be a future. And that was the problem. She enjoyed being with Tim, but was it a strong enough foundation on which to build a lifetime's relationship? Was that really what she wanted? She sat back, comb in hand. Sometimes it was. There were days when she was tempted, even despite that slightly irresponsible attitude of Tim's which irritated her, perhaps more than it should. But that in itself was perhaps another reason for her hesitation. What merely irritated now might become unbearable after they were married, especially when she took her own work so seriously. Which only made it all the more depressing that she seemed to clash so often, temperamentally, with Oliver Steele.

She blinked as she realised she had been sitting staring into space and that the doorbell was ringing furiously signalling Tim's early arrival.

Grabbing a coat and bag she ran to the door reluctant for some reason to invite him into the flat. What she needed was a change of surroundings, somewhere away from the smell of hospitals, even the talk of hospitals. An evening without complications and thoughts of the senior consultant. He was becoming far too persistent an intruder into her life in more ways than one, she decided, and it was time she put him firmly in his place.

Perhaps more of her resolve lingered than she realised because she returned Tim's kiss of greeting rather more enthusiastically than usual and consequently invited an embrace which had her drawing away breathlessly when he finally, and with obvious reluctance, released her.

'Mm, that was very nice and you look gorgeous. I've missed you. Do you really want to go out or should we stay in and share a more intimate evening together on your sofa?' He nibbled teasingly at her ear and she wriggled warily away from his arms, almost glad of the few spots of rain which gave her an excuse to suggest they head for the car.

'I don't really fancy an evening in, to be honest. Do you mind if we go out somewhere, if only for an hour? I'm actually quite tired but I need to unwind.'

He released her, looking faintly disgruntled. 'There are times when I need to unwind too, you know, Sara. A man needs to know where he stands and, frankly, I never do these days when I'm with you.'

Taken completely by surprise she stared at him for a moment, feeling her eyes prick with unexpected tears. 'I'm sorry . . . Would you rather we just left going out for tonight? I'm afraid I'm not very good company.'

'Oh for heaven's sake. I didn't say that.' He was blustering a little and she knew that he was annoyed as he opened the car door and she climbed in, forcing herself to relax as she turned to stare out of the window. There was something different about

Tim tonight, about his mood. She could sense it without being able to put her finger precisely on it. There had been a kind of intensity in the kiss which had never been there before. Or again, was the change in herself? She swallowed hard. Perhaps it was just that they were both over-tired.

'How are you getting on with the new senior consultant now?' she asked conversationally, simply to break the silence.

He swore softly under his breath as the traffic lights changed and he had to bring the car to a halt. Watching him, Sara wondered at the sudden tension in his face. There was an edginess about him which was certainly something new, even though he spoke casually enough as the car moved forward again.

'I suppose we get along, just about. It's no good pretending I like the fellow. He's too damned arrogant for a start. Far too sure of himself.'

'Is that so unusual in senior consultants?' Sara managed to smile. 'Not the arrogance, I just mean that . . . well I suppose they have to have rather more self-confidence than most in order to do the job.'

'Oh I see. Become an expert on senior consultants all of a sudden have you?'

There was just the faintest trace of malice in the words and she flinched. 'No, not exactly,' she managed to say evenly. 'It's just that . . . well I've seen him on the wards and he's obviously very capable and the patients certainly all seem to respond well to him. Surely that's what counts.'

'I suppose it is. I just didn't get the impression you'd taken to him either, that's all. Obviously I was wrong.' He flung a sidelong glance in her direction and she was glad of the fading light which hid the faint colour which surged into her cheeks.

'No, as a matter of fact, I don't particularly like him, but in our job we can't really resort to personalities, can we? We both have to work with the man, like it or not.'

'Yes, well I suppose some of us do. But perhaps not for longer than necessary.'

He made no attempt to elaborate and the words left her feeling vaguely worried. However she didn't feel inclined to press the matter, not when he was in his present mood. They fell into an uneasy silence and it was a relief when they reached the pub. It was one they often used, mainly because it wasn't over-frequented by staff from the hospital, but she found herself wondering if it might not have been better after all if they had been part of a crowd.

They walked into the warmth of the pub. A log fire blazed at one end of the room and they gravitated naturally towards it, as most other people had apparently done, now that summer seemed finally to have vanished. Tim disappeared to the bar for drinks, leaving her to sit at the table staring contemplatively into the flames. The smell and the sound of crackling wood conjured up other tantalising images, of home, peace, comfort, her father . . . Oliver Steele.

She shook herself mentally and rallied herself to

be cheerful and more attentive as Tim returned, placing the usual glass of Coke in front of her and taking a long swallow at his own drink. It surprised her a little to see that it was a large whisky because he usually rarely drank anything stronger than a single spirit or a pint of beer when he had to be on duty the following morning. She opened her mouth to comment then bit the words back—after all he was an adult and perfectly able to decide for himself.

'It's nice and cosy in here isn't it?' She drove a note of cheerfulness into her voice and was relieved to see him respond, probably hating the atmophere between them every bit as much as she did.

'Mm.' He sat on the seat beside her. 'There's something about the smell of wood smoke. Do you remember when we came here last Christmas? The whole place was decorated with holly and ivy.'

She did remember and smiled. Everything had been so much less complicated then. Or was it perhaps just that she had been incredibly naïve, imagining they could go on for ever as they were? If so, she knew that the illusion was about to be shattered as Tim took her hand in his and stared at her fingers. With an uneasy sense of premonition she knew what was coming and wished he hadn't chosen now, not tonight.

'I'm sorry if I seem like a bear with a sore head. It's just that . . . well, I've been trying all day to work out the best way to ask you to marry me.' He looked at her and must have seen the sudden look of wary resistance in her eyes. 'Sara, you must know it's been in my mind for a long time. I've made it pretty clear so it can't come as any surprise to you.'

She struggled hard to find something to say, something which wouldn't sound utterly heartless.

'Oh, Tim.'

'Well, it doesn't, does it?'

She shook her head, conscious of a sudden tightness in her throat. 'No, I suppose not. But why is it suddenly so important now?'

'Damn it, Sara,' his jaw tightened, 'why not now? When would be a more convenient time? This year, next year, sometime . . . or never?' He broke off, releasing her hand abruptly, and drained his glass in one swallow. 'I feel as if you're playing some kind of game with me, Sara. I thought . . . well I know nothing was ever definite but I imagined we had some kind of understanding. Or am I being too old fashioned?' His lips twisted bitterly.

'No, oh no.'

'Then what, Sara? Look, I need to know where I stand. If there *is* any kind of future in this, for me.' He frowned down at his empty glass. 'I need to get my life settled, Sara, to know where I'm going, both in my job and personally. I can't wait for ever, living in hopes. If there's no point to it then I'd rather know.'

She stared at him unhappily. 'You make it sound as if you're afraid of wasting time.'

'Well aren't I doing just that, Sara, where you're concerned?' She saw the slight colour stain his neck. 'I can go a long way in my career, Sara, and

I'm still old fashioned enough to believe that in the medical profession a man is more highly regarded if he was a wife. Particularly one who . . .' He broke off and she stared at him.

'Particularly one who what?'

He seemed oddly discomfited. 'Well I wasn't going to say it, but being who you are . . .'

She drew in a harsh, painful breath and said quietly, 'Don't you mean who my father is, Tim? I'm sorry, but you of all people must know I've never traded upon the relationship and I don't intend to start now, not even for you.' The mere idea, the thought that he had even considered it, shocked her so much that she had to blink away the tears which threatened suddenly.

He put his glass down with an impatient oath. 'For God's sake, don't put words into my mouth. I wasn't thinking any such thing. The thought never even crossed my mind. Surely you know me better than that? I was going to say particularly a wife who has some experience of the work herself, who knows what it involves, the strain, the hours.'

He looked so much like a child suddenly deprived of a favourite toy that she regretted the words and could have bitten out her tongue for having said what she did. Perhaps she had jumped to the wrong conclusion. They were both on edge tonight for some reason. Whatever the cause she felt too weary to argue and, in a way, she felt sorry for Tim. It might have been better if she had broken off their relationship some time ago. Before it had reached this stage.

'Oh Tim, I'm sorry. It's just that . . . I wasn't expecting a proposal tonight, out of the blue, I suppose. I'm tired and I can't think straight.'

His mouth tightened angrily. 'Does it really need so much thought?'

'Yes, I rather think it does. It's an important decision. Probably the most important of my life . . . our lives. Don't you see that?'

'I don't have any doubts. We get on well together, most of the time.'

'But that's just the point. Is most of the time enough? Marriage is for ever, Tim, at least it is as far as I'm concerned, so I have to be sure.' Instinctively she reached out to touch his hand. 'I am fond of you, Tim, very fond, but it wouldn't be fair to you either if I said I'd marry you if there was even the slightest chance that it might not work.' She withdrew her hand. Or did he draw away from her? She wasn't sure. 'Will you give me a little longer to think about it? I promise I will think about it, but tonight I'm too tired.'

Ungraciously he refused to look at her. Perhaps she shouldn't blame him, not when in her own heart she had the suspicion that if she really did love him she wouldn't have needed any time at all.

He got to his feet without answering and went to the bar to order another drink, returning to sit toying with the glass almost as if he needed to occupy his hands. Anything rather than look directly at her. It occurred to her that there was even an element of guilt in the way he was behaving, yet surely she should be the one experiencing that particular emotion?

Looking at him, sitting so taut and hunched over the table, she almost changed her mind and said yes there and then. Only the belief that it would be foolish to make such an important decision while she was feeling drained and bad tempered and so unsure gave her the courage to stick to her guns. After all, tomorrow was another day. Was it so much to ask, when her answer might affect the rest of her life?

As much to dissuade him, tactfully, not to drink any more as because she was suddenly eager to get back to the peaceful solitude of her flat, she said gently, 'Perhaps if I'm going to do that serious thinking I'd better be getting home. In any case, we're both on duty in the morning.' She was on her feet while he still stared moodily into his glass.

'As long as you realise I can't wait for ever, Sara. I meant what I said. I need to know fairly soon.'

For a moment she stood motionless, a feeling of vague panic tightening her throat. 'Why is time suddenly so important?'

He looked at her, then away again. 'I suppose you have to know sooner or later. I'm thinking of applying for a new job. I've had it just about up to here with Clem's.' He got unsteadily to his feet and it was some seconds before she could bring herself to speak.

'And just when had you planned to tell me about this new job, Tim? After I'd said I would marry you, or was it to be a surprise?' She felt angry, and retaliated with a vehemence which left her shaking.

'Oh come on, Sara, you can't have your cake and eat it. You've known for a long time that I wasn't happy at Clem's. The new job wasn't an ultimatum if that's what you mean.'

'Wasn't it, Tim?' She was breathing hard. 'It sounded remarkably like it.'

'Well if that's how you want to see it, that's up to you but you can't seriously expect me to hang around here for ever, can you?'

She had to swallow hard to get rid of the lump in her throat as she said quietly. 'No, I don't suppose I can. Just where is this job and when exactly do you need an answer?'

He brushed the back of his hand across his mouth. 'It's in Canada and I have to make the decision within the next two weeks, so it's up to you, Sara.'

'Canada?' The colour drained from her face and her hand reached out for the support of the chair. It was almost like looking at a stranger, she thought. 'You mean, with or without me, you're going. That's it, isn't it, Tim?'

'I'm hoping it will be with you, Sara, but it's up to you.'

For some seconds she stood with hands clenched, trying desperately to clear her brain, to think straight. But all she felt was very tired and cold and oddly detached.

'Well, in that case it looks as if I'm going to have to do some even harder thinking, doesn't it?'

Without answering he made for the door and she

followed blindly out to the car park, waiting as he fumbled for the keys. He dropped them and for the first time she realised his hands were shaking.

'Shall I drive?'

'For God's sake, I'm not drunk if that's what you mean. I'm quite capable of getting you back in one piece if that's what's worrying you.'

She bit her lip, knowing that to reason with him would be useless. In any case she wasn't absolutely sure how much he had had to drink. It may well have been tiredness which was making him irritable and clumsy.

She got into the car, sitting silently as he climbed in beside her. They exchanged only a few perfunctory remarks as he drove. Once, as he took a bend in the road too sharply, her hand came up but she just managed not to cry out or grasp his arm. Tim seemed totally unaware of what had happened.

It was as they neared the flat, turning from a small, minor road on to the busy main one, that her fears were realised. She saw the other car only seconds before they plunged, headlong, into it. She was even aware that she screamed and saw the look of horror on Tim's face as he tried desperately to wrench the wheel over. But it was too late. The inevitability of what happened was like a nightmare, totally beyond her control. She heard the screech of breaks, felt a jarring blow on her temple as the car spun wildly out of control, and was vaguely surprised to feel the thin trickle of blood running down her face before lights flashed and she was tumbling into a black whirling pool.

CHAPTER NINE

It was the voice which brought her back to reality. She had been lying there, listening to it droning relentlessly in the background, angrily resenting the intrusion it made into her consciousness, and even more so the hands which, though blissfully cool and gentle, persisted in probing areas of pain of which she was slowly, miserably, becoming aware.

'Right, I think another suture here, Sister, then that should do it. She's lucky. There won't be a scar. Good, fine . . . a swab here to get rid of some of that gunge.' Then a blurred face was bending lower, so close that it was almost touching hers. 'Mm, not as bad as it looks, thank God.'

Sara fought the uncomfortably new stinging sensation at her temple until a strong hand caught and held her own protesting ones and a voice said gently but firmly, 'It's all right, Sara. We've had to put a few stitches in a head wound but it isn't serious. You can relax.'

She thought she heard him add softly, 'my love,' but the room was spinning and she felt far too tired to do anything except give way to the few tears which slipped weakly on to her cheek as her hands were released. Then the voice, distinctly more cool, said, 'All right, Sister, I've done everything I can do. I'd better go and check on the other patient. Will you carry on here?'

It was the familiarity of those voices which finally made her drag her eyes open, then it was several seconds before her gaze focused on a face which she recognised, slowly, as that of Sister Casualty.

Berenice Williams smiled reassuringly. 'Hello, nice to see you're back with us. How are you feeling?'

How *was* she feeling? Sara frowned. Her brain felt oddly detached from the rest of her body but she was gradually becoming aware of a painful throbbing somewhere and the rest of her seemed to ache. Her fingers probed the wound at her temple and she winced.

'I wouldn't do that,' Sister Williams advised with gentle humour. 'Someone has gone to the trouble of doing some very delicate embroidery on it and he isn't going to be pleased if you undo all his good work.' She turned away briefly. 'Thank you, Nurse, you can remove the trolley now and ring Women's Med will you? Offer my apologies and say I'm sending them another patient.'

Her attractively slim figure moved about the curtained cubicle, then she came to take Sara's pulse, holding her wrist in her cool fingers and studying her fob-watch for a few seconds while she looked down at her. She was smiling but her astute gaze was also registering the gradual but definite return of colour. 'Well that's rather better than it was when they brought you in. I must say when I saw it was you I could hardly believe my eyes. We'd been warned to expect two admissions but we didn't have any information.' She stopped, her face becoming serious. 'I don't suppose you remember much about it, do you?'

Sara had been lying there, frantically trying to fit the pieces of a jigsaw together. If only her head would stop aching so that she could think. 'I was in a car . . .'

'That's right. And you were involved in a bit of an accident, but there's no real damage done, thank goodness. You have a slight concussion and a small wound which needed a few stitches, but you're lucky, it won't even leave a scar. By tomorrow you'll probably have bruises in places you didn't even know you had places, but a couple of days in bed and you'll be feeling much better.'

It was the kind of reassurance Sara herself had given so many times to anxious patients and relatives. She had an added advantage in that experience told her it was true and yet, somewhere deep in the recesses of her mind, something wouldn't let her relax and give way to the exhausted sleep she longed for. There was something else. Something . . . No, not something, someone. There had been someone else in the car with her. The colour drained from her face again. 'Tim, oh God, where is he? Is he . . .?'

'No, now don't get yourself into a fret.' Sara wasn't aware of the slight tightening of the other girl's lips or the note of displeasure in her voice. 'Everything is under control. Dr Lawson is in one of the other cubicles and is being attended to now.

You were lucky, both of you. We've been rushed off our feet here tonight. We had a pile-up between a bus and a car and all of them were brought here. We've had staff rushing in all directions and doctors coming in when they were supposed to be off duty. Even Mr Steele helped. In fact it's him you have to thank for that piece of needlework. Believe me, if some of our housemen had tackled it I wouldn't have given much for your chances of getting away without at least some scarring, but Mr Steele wouldn't let anyone near. He took over completely and I must say it's a real privilege to see such patience and concentration.'

Sara closed her eyes, hearing sister's voice drone on, letting a whole gamut of emotions wash over her. Oliver Steele himself had attended to her. That explained of course the voice which had seemed so familiar. What it didn't explain was why the memory of his hands, moving with infinite gentleness over her body, should suddenly bring her ridiculously close to tears.

'Of course, it's marvellous the way staff rally when it's one of their own. But you must have seen it yourself as well, the way everyone closes ranks to help.'

Berenice Williams' voice brought her, shaking, back to reality and the knowledge that she was right. That was precisely what had happened. She and Tim had been recognised as staff and Oliver Steele had just happened to be around. Suddenly she didn't want to think about it any more.

'Where is Tim? How is he?'

'I've told you, he's in one of the other cubicles being attended to right now. As to how he is, I'm afraid I don't know.' She saw the look on Sara's face. 'No, really, I'm not keeping anything from you. You must know yourself that until a full examination has been done there's no point in making guesses. As soon as we have any news I'll let you know, I promise.'

'Was he . . . did he seem badly hurt?'

'He was unconscious, but that's all I know. Now why don't you try to get some sleep. We're having you moved up to Women's Med. They're pretty full but you'll be put into one of the side rooms so you should be able to rest undisturbed until the hordes of visitors and well-wishers start popping in.' Sister grinned ruefully. 'That's one of the penalties of working in a job like ours, I suppose. Anyway, I must be off. With a bit of luck I might even be able to take a coffee break now that the rush has died down. Anyway, best of luck. Ah, here are the porters.'

She stood aside and Sara felt herself being lifted gently on to a trolley and lay staring up at the ceiling as they wheeled her out of Casualty, into a lift and then along the corridor to Women's Med. It was strange how things which had always seemed so familiar could now look so different.

Night sister on Women's Med came to meet the trolley. It was pleasantly reassuring to recognise Lisa Carson with whom she had gone through PTS. In no time at all she was tucked up in bed, the staff moving quietly and efficiently around her and, to her relief. no one made any attempt to question her or talk to her.

'Just relax and get some sleep,' the navy-clad figure murmured, and Sara was happy to do just that. giving way to the exhaustion which was claiming her and the effects of the tablets she had been given down in Casualty, except that her brain didn't seem to want to relax.

She wondered where Tim was. What was happening to him? How badly hurt was he? She closed her eyes, moaning softly as a brief memory of another car and Tim's ashen face as he fought to avoid it flooded into her mind. They had been arguing, she remembered, and Tim had been drinking. If only she hadn't let him drive. If he died it would be her fault. Surely there was something she could have done to prevent it, her befuddled brain insisted. But as she finally fell asleep, she wasn't at all sure what that something was.

When she opened her eyes again, it was to see Oliver Steele standing beside the bed, looking down at her with so grim an expression that she immediately feared the worst.

'Tim.' She sat up quickly, only to subside again weakly as her skull felt like it was being pounded with a mallet.

'Relax. I've not come to tell you he's dead. On the contrary, young Lawson escaped remarkably lightly . . . under the circumstances. Far more lightly than he deserved, in my opinion.'

Sara felt the relief flood through her. Relief

which was all too obvious to the man watching her, and who placed his own, albeit inaccurate interpretation on it.

There were dark smudges beneath her eyes as she stared up at him. 'How is he? When will I be allowed to see him? I suppose he must be on Men's Medical.' She added the latter almost as an afterthought to herself, unaware that she frowned.

It was odd how the last few hours, even though they had been confused in most respects, had made her see far more clearly that she didn't love Tim and probably never had, not really. She was glad he hadn't been badly hurt. The fact that he had brought what happened upon himself scarcely even seemed relevant, but it didn't blind her, either, to the fact that, yesterday, she had seen a side of him which she had never seen before, and she hadn't liked what she had seen. As to how she would tell him she couldn't marry him, or even when . . . obviously it was going to have to wait until he was fully recovered.

For some reason, only then did the waiting man's words fully penetrate her brain and her gaze rose, sharply, to his.

'Under what circumstances?' Her voice sounded sharp, edgy. Just how much did he know? With a sudden feeling of panic she realised how bad things would be for Tim if it got out that he had been drinking and driving. Not only his job but his whole future would be on the line. A wide range of emotions flickered across her face before Oliver Steele coldly said, 'I think you know perfectly well

what I'm talking about, Sister, and I'd be grateful if
you didn't treat me like a naïve adolescent. Lawson
had been drinking and there's no point denying it. I
could smell it on him as soon as I got near him, and
my guess is that he'd had quite a few.' Sara flinched
at the sudden sneer in his voice as he asked, 'What
was it, some kind of celebration? If so, I hope the
occasion was something special and we're not likely
to be getting any repeat performances.'

She stared at him, too numbed for the moment to
speak, then she said, incredulously, 'You mean . . .
you don't intend reporting Tim? Even though you
know?'

'Oh don't get me wrong,' the strong mouth
curled contemptuously, 'I'm not staying silent out
of any gallant motive. Believe me I wouldn't consider Lawson's departure any great loss to this
hospital.'

She gasped. 'You have no right to say that just
because you happen to dislike Tim.'

'My dear Miss West, you seem to presume that
my judgment of Dr Lawson is based upon something entirely personal, but I assure you that isn't
the case.' The steel-cold eyes narrowed as he
looked at her. 'I simply happen to think it will avoid
a great deal of unpleasantness for a great many
people if we can avoid the kind of publicity which
would be inevitable if it were to get around that one
of the doctors is a drunken driver. As far as I'm
concerned, Lawson's imminent departure can only
be good news.'

Shock held her rigid as she tried to take in the

words. He knew that Tim intended leaving. None of it made sense. The only thing she knew for certain was that it was hardly surprising Tim had been so edgy lately, if this was the kind of pressure he had been under, and yet, even as words rose to her lips in his defence, she bit them back. Tim had been drunk. She had tried to stop him driving, but perhaps she hadn't tried hard enough.

She licked her dry lips, all too conscious of Oliver Steele's looming presence. A tear welled up and she quickly blinked it away, wishing he would just leave her alone instead of glaring at her as if she were to blame for what had happened. 'I have a headache,' she muttered feebly, hoping it might persuade him to go. But to her chagrin, he stood his ground.

'You're damn lucky that's all you have. His strong hands were suddenly gripping her arms and she gasped at the fury in his voice. 'I don't suppose it has even occurred to you, you little idiot, that you might have been killed. My God, when I saw them bring you in I thought . . .'

She was never to know what he thought because his mouth closed on hers in a kiss which seemed to drive the breath out of her lungs. There wasn't even time to respond because as quickly as it had begun, the assault upon her emotions ended, leaving her feeling breathless and, for some reason, bitterly frustrated. She saw the angry pulse hammering in his neck as he released her abruptly.

'My God, Sara, I swear if you ever . . .'

She wanted to ask why he was so angry, what she

had done that could possibly justify the savagery she saw in his eyes, but even as her mouth opened he had turned and walked out of the room and she was left staring miserably at the closed door.

For a long time she lay thinking about it until her head really did ache and she felt too tired to try and analyse the reasons any longer. In any case, it was pretty obvious, she concluded before she fell into a deep, dreamless sleep. The only thing Mr Oliver Steele was worried about was his precious hospital and its good name. So why had he kissed her? She let the question go, too tired to pursue it, but the last thought to flash into her mind before she finally gave way to sleep was that she couldn't possibly marry Tim because, like an idiot, she was in love with someone else. The fact that that someone else had made it perfectly clear that he had no time for her whatsoever was something she was going to have to learn to live with, and that wasn't going to be easy. In fact, it was going to be impossible.

CHAPTER TEN

MUCH to her annoyance it was two days before Sara found herself allowed up, and then only because she had played down the remnants of a headache and had smilingly managed to reassure John Sinclair that she was feeling much better.

'I feel such a fraud lying here,' she insisted, 'especially when I know how short-staffed we are. It's not even as if I suffered any serious damage.'

'My dear girl, you of all people should know better than to dismiss any head injury lightly. Is this how you would advise your patients?'

'But I'm not a patient,' she smiled up at him. In his sixties and grey-haired, John Sinclair was popular with all members of staff and she had always found him easy to get on with. 'In any case, I have my experience to tell me that I'm perfectly capable of going back to work.'

'Hm, well you still look a little peaky to me.'

'I expect some fresh air would soon put that right.'

He didn't answer as his fingers clasped her wrist and he checked her pulse before saying grudgingly, 'Yes, well that seems all right, and the temperature looks normal.' He consulted the chart and a mischievous twinkle in his eye told her that he was purposely teasing her. 'Well, I don't suppose I have any real objections, provided you're sensible, mind. Delegate for a while. Don't do what you don't have to.'

'I'm sure there's absolutely no danger of that.'

'And if I believed that for one moment I certainly wouldn't be having any doubts about letting you go, young woman. Still, if you feel up to it you can get back to work in a couple of days.'

As she got dressed she wasn't at all sure that she hadn't perhaps been a little hasty after all. Her legs felt decidedly wobbly but forty-eight hours spent pottering quietly in the flat before she went back on duty would probably do her far more good than lying in bed with too many uncomfortable thoughts for company.

It was only now that she fully appreciated just how long the days were for patients confined to bed, although she hadn't been short of visitors popping in and out to see how she was, bringing her flowers and fruit which she hadn't felt like eating. To begin with all she had wanted was to lie there letting the silence drift over her, and then, as the headache had eased, she had begun to think about Tim, half expecting to see him come through the door at any moment, his usual cheerful self.

But he hadn't come and then she had started to worry. Perhaps he was more badly hurt than they had let her believe. It was Jane Barratt, calling in on her way off duty, who quickly quashed the notion.

'Good heavens, no. Have you been lying here worrying about him?' She perched on the edge of the bed, keeping a wary eye out for Sister. 'They kept him on Men's Med overnight of course, but he was allowed to go next morning. Actually he got off remarkably lightly, with just a slight bump on his head which needed a couple of stitches, and shock. I thought you knew.' She glanced shrewdly at her friend's white face, seeing the look which flickered briefly in the grey-green eyes, and said brightly, 'I expect he would have come in but he was back on duty and probably hasn't had the chance.'

'Yes, I expect you're right.' And yet surely if he had wanted to come, if he had really been interested, he would have made time, a little voice added. She turned her head away lethargically, feeling vaguely hurt until it occurred to her that she hadn't seen anything of Oliver Steele either. Not that there was any earthly reason why she should have, she told herself crossly. After all, the senior consultant was hardly likely to visit a sister just because of a bump on the head. All the same, she couldn't help thinking that it was rather more than her head which had been affected by the accident.

In the event she was more than happy to get back to work. Forty-eight hours of her own company, listening for a telephone which stubbornly refused to ring, had given her too much opportunity to think, and her thoughts had been far from comfortable.

Sooner or later she was going to have to see Tim. Perhaps he was avoiding her purposely now in order to give her time to think. It was ironic really, she sighed. Yesterday everything had seemed so simple. Today she wasn't so sure. Had she been entirely fair in coming to a decision based upon a side of Tim she had seen without knowing at the time the kind of pressure he was under?

Sitting on her favourite window-seat, a hand tucked under her chin, she sighed. 'I'm behaving like an adolescent,' she thought, finding the knowledge disquieting because she had always considered herself such a practical person, and any practical person would have known exactly what to do.

Her arrival back on the ward was greeted by cheers from the patients, who had obviously heard about the accident, and with relief by Jane who put a cup of coffee on the desk in front of her the moment Sara reached the office.

'Mm, just what I needed. How did you know?'

'It was a calculated guess. In any case, it's a sort of welcome-back gesture.'

'Oh dear, that sounds ominous. Do I take it we have problems?'

'No, not really. Just that we had Batty Binford wished on to us while you were off and she and I just don't seem to hit it off somehow.'

Sara chuckled. 'I think I know what you mean. I'm sure she's a first class sister, but she does tend to regard the ward as something of an army parade-ground.'

'You can say that again. We practically stood to attention for morning report. All I can say is, thank heavens you were only off for two days. Mind you,' she continued, giving a long hard look at Sara's face, 'you're still looking very pale. Are you sure you're really up to it yet?'

'Now don't you start.' Sara drained her coffee and looked at her watch. 'And talking of morning report, isn't it time we got cracking? Otherwise we'll be going at full gallop for the rest of the day, trying to catch up.'

'Actually there's not a great deal to report. Young Gary Blackford went home, convinced that every female within a ten-mile radius is going to be a pushover now that he has his new ears, as he calls them.'

Sara laughed. 'And he's probably right. He really is quite a nice looking lad.'

'I know, but I felt he had quite enough confidence in his own popularity for me to tell him so. No decent, self-respecting nurse has been safe this last few days. By the way, have you heard from Tim?'

Sara's smile vanished. 'No, as a matter of fact I haven't.'

'Oh dear, what about your beautiful friendship? Do I detect a note of sourness in your voice?'

Sara got to her feet and crossed to the large filing cabinet. 'I suppose you could say that.'

'But I thought everything was going so well. I mean everyone's been half expecting an announcement for ages now.'

Sara bit her lip. 'Yes, well, that's just it. Everyone has taken it for granted but suddenly when Tim asked me to marry him, I just knew . . . I couldn't do it. At least,' she shook her head, 'I'm supposed to be thinking it over. I am very fond of him.'

Jane pulled a face. 'Fond isn't exactly how you should feel about the man you're going to marry. It's hardly enough, is it?'

'That's what I've been telling myself.'

'And the problem, I take it, is telling Tim?'

Sara looked at her in troubled silence for a minute. 'I just wish I could be absolutely sure. In a way I feel so guilty. I mean we've been going out together for ages.' She wondered vaguely why Jane suddenly seemed to avoid her gaze, then told herself she had imagined it as her friend said brightly, 'Well, perhaps that's the trouble. You need a break from each other. Besides, Tim Lawson isn't the only fish in the sea you know. Or hadn't you noticed? Take our dishy Mr Steele for instance.'

Sara's lips compressed as she swept a pile of case notes up and said briskly, knowing that her cheeks were a darker shade of pink, 'No, thank you. I have the feeling that I'd be way out of my depth there. In any case, he's more my idea of a shark.' And she reached hurriedly for the phone as it started to ring, leaving the other girl to study her with a look of surprised curiosity.

It was a hectic morning and they were all kept on their toes as patients went up to theatre and returned later, needing the careful attention of regular checks to see that they were recovering satisfactorily. Several patients were down for discharge but it seemed their beds had scarcely been stripped and re-made before a new patient was admitted for urgent abdominal surgery the following day.

The hands of the clock moved relentlessly on.

'Nurse, you need an identiband for the new patient.' Sara's eyes scanned the trolley. 'Right, fix the TPR chart to the foot of the bed until required. We shall need a drawsheet, and have the elevator blocks ready, just in case we need to raise the bed.'

The girl sped away and so it went on. There was scarcely time to think as they went relentlessly through the day's routine, but Sara still managed to find herself dreading the afternoon when Oliver Steele would be doing his round. There was no way she could avoid it because Jane Barratt had gone off duty at one o'clock and in any case, as she told herself firmly, she couldn't go on avoiding him for ever.

As it happened, however, he wasn't the first person to arrive. She was making notes for the new admission when the office door opened and she looked up impatiently at the disturbance to see Tim standing sheepishly in the doorway.

It was odd to find herself looking at him as if expecting to find something changed, but nothing had.

'Hi. Should I throw my hat in first, or is it safe to come in?'

For some reason she found herself failing to respond to his attempt at humour. The tardiness of his concern for her after the accident must have gone deeper than she had realised, and to find him grinning at her now, as if nothing had happened, made her speak more sharply even than she had intended.

'I'm afraid I don't have time to play games, Tim.' She looked pointedly at her watch. 'We have ward round in ten minutes. But then you should know that.' She looked at him directly. 'Aren't you supposed to be accompanying Mr Steele? I thought it was his practice to have his team with him when he sees patients who are due for op.'

'Oh that's okay,' he said, seeming unrepentant. 'I can hop in at the end of the line when they arrive. The great man won't even notice.'

'I wouldn't be so sure,' Sara muttered under her breath as she collected a file and deposited it in the appropriate trolley. Somehow she couldn't imagine anything escaping Oliver Steele's canny gaze.

Tim caught hold of her arm, drawing her to a halt as she would have slipped past him to get to the desk. 'I came to see how you are, and to apologise.'

'Well as you can see, I'm fine.' She forced a thin smile as his gaze took in the faint shadows beneath her eyes.

'I did mean to come and see you. It's just that . . . well I felt so rotten about what happened.' He brushed a hand across his eyes. 'In fact I don't really know what happened.'

She felt like saying that she knew very well, that he had had too much to drink. But it seemed pointless and, judging from his haggard expression, he had suffered enough. She moved restlessly beneath the pressure of his restraining hand on her arm.

'I'm sorry, Tim, I really do have a lot to do.'

'All right. I realise we can't talk now but will you see me later? I think there are things we have to say, Sara. Things we need to get straight.' He let her go reluctantly. 'I'm still hoping you'll say you'll marry me, and you did say you'd give me an answer.'

She cut him off, knowing that she was being deliberately ruthless: 'I've scarcely had a chance to think about anything, Tim.'

'But you will, won't you, and . . . well you won't let your answer be coloured by what's happened, will you?' he pleaded. 'I know I was a damned fool but surely what we have together is too good to throw away.'

She brushed a strand of hair from her eyes, wondering exactly what it was that she and Tim did have, what they had ever had. There was no time to think about it as, through the window of the small office, she saw her third year nurse, Lindsay Forbes, gesticulating wildly as the ward doors swung open and, with a gasp, Sara headed swiftly for the door.

'Oh no, he's here, and he's early. For heaven's sake Tim, unless you want to find yourself in more trouble you'd better get out there.'

She needn't have worried. He slipped past her on to the ward as she made her way, heart thudding, towards the tall figure, sweeping the pile of case notes from Nurse Forbes' hands as she did so. How typical of him to be early, she thought crossly, but her voice was its usual briskly formal self as she said

'Good morning, Sir. Is there any particular patient you wish to see first?'

For a moment the dark eyes narrowed as he took the notes from her hand. 'Should you be back on duty so soon, Sister?'

'I'm perfectly recovered, thank you, Sir, and Mr Sinclair gave his approval.'

He made a noise which sounded extraordinarily like a grunt, but he was already immersed, frowning deeply, in the patient's notes, and she had the dampening feeling that she had already been dismissed completely from his mind.

To her relief she saw that Tim had managed to sneak in amongst the crowd of medical students gradually making their way on to the ward and towards the first bed. Catching her eye he winked and she found herself thinking furiously that there were times when Tim's light-hearted attitude to everything was sadly misplaced. Or was she being too prudish? But she had always felt that medicine required a rather more mature attitude than the one Tim often gave to it. Oh well, she sighed, as usual he had got away with it.

The illusion was swiftly banished, however, as Oliver Steele's dark head rose and his glance swept the group circled about him and came to rest on the grinning figure. 'Ah, Dr Lawson, how good of you to join us. I apologise if we have called you away from more important matters.' The gaze flickered maliciously in her own direction and Sara felt herself blush. 'But now that you're here, perhaps you could give us the benefit of your time and talent and take us through this first case.' He handed the folder to Tim who took it, looking, Sara noted, slightly sheepish. 'Mr Dunford, as you know of course, had his operation several days ago. Carry on, Doctor, please.'

It was all more of a nightmare than Sara had anticipated. Her hands shook as she helped the patient to unfasten his pyjamas for the examination and when it was finished, helped him to settle comfortably again. Her only consolation was that Tim coped splendidly. But then he should, she thought, with a hint of annoyance, because Jane Barratt had informed her that he had seen the patient only the previous afternoon and had spent some time chatting with him about cars.

Even so, she couldn't help smiling at the look of smug satisfaction on his face as Oliver Steele made no comment and they all progressed to the next bed.

By the time they had made their way half-way round the ward her head was aching and she was having to concentrate all her attention on what was being said and what was required of her. Not for the first time she was glad of Nurse Forbes' quiet efficiency, which ensured that the necessary trolleys were on hand the minute they were required for specific examinations, but also that the case notes were handed firmly into her grasp. That was just as well since her own hands were shaking and her eyes seemed incapable of focussing clearly on anything. It must be delayed shock, she told herself, feeling the clammy heat of her forehead. She straightened up instinctively as she became aware of the look of irritation on Oliver Steele's face as his gaze rested on her, briefly, before he turned away.

The last patient had been admitted two days earlier, transferred from Men's Medical, and was to undergo operation as soon as his general condition had improved sufficiently to enable him to stand it. He was certainly very ill and Sara felt her heart contract as she looked down at the man, knowing that even if he did survive surgery there was still only perhaps a ten per cent chance that he would make a complete recovery.

She handed the slim file to Oliver Steele, trying not to betray the fact that even the brief contact her fingers made against his sent a kind of shock running through her.

She noticed with idle curiosity the way his thick eyelashes curled as he read the notes, jerking her gaze away as he looked up and announced that he intended making a brief examination. She slipped back the bedcovers and watched as he took infinite care, trying to cause the patient as little discomfort and inconvenience as possible. He straightened up and took the notes from her again. He looked tired, she thought, seeing the tiny lines which seemed to have appeared in his face.

'I'd like to see the results of the blood tests, Sister.'

She blinked. 'I'm sorry, sir?'

'The blood tests. I ordered then when I made my last examination.'

She stared at him, realising that something was expected of her. 'But . . . surely they must be with the rest of the notes?'

'If they were, Sister, I should hardly need to ask for them. Take a look for yourself.'

She did so, flipping through the pages before returning her gaze helplessly to his. 'I'm afraid I don't understand. If they were done, the notes should be here. They are always put straight into the appropriate file and checked.' Her voice faded as she frowned, some awful premonition already dawning as she said falteringly, 'I'm afraid I don't see any record of the tests having been done.' Without being aware of it her sickened gaze flew to Tim. It would have been his responsibility to see to it. He, of all people, must know the importance of such tests. Surely he couldn't have overlooked something so vital?

She didn't need to ask the question aloud. The answer was written guiltily all over his face and she had to turn away, fighting the wave of nausea which threatened to envelop her. Even worse, she heard him already making excuses, and she couldn't bear to see him, blustering and red-faced.

'I don't see how it could have happened. But of course I was off duty personally at the time. I suppose that must have been it. I gave orders to Dr Richards . . .'

Sara had never seen such cold fury as she saw now on Oliver Steele's taut face. Without a word he moved away from the bedside, flicking aside the curtains where he waited until Tim joined him, out of the patient's earshot. He was breathing hard Sara noticed, and she couldn't help feeling a twinge of pity for Tim.

'I don't accept the fact that you were off duty as any excuse, Lawson. The responsibility was ultimately yours, not that of a houseman, and you know it. Those blood tests were vital. You must have been aware of it and now, as a result of this delay, a seriously ill patient may have to wait for his operation.'

It was obvious from the pulsing of the nerve in Mr Steele's jaw that he was battling with himself to keep his anger contained. Miserably, she found herself unable to look at Tim, neither wanting to witness his embarrassment nor wanting to hear him try to excuse the inexcusable.

Without thinking she said, quietly. 'Perhaps if we take the sample now, Sir, I can carry it down to the lab personally and get them to rush it through. We may still be able to go ahead.'

She felt Oliver Steele's attention diverted briefly from Tim's ashen face to her own and thought she detected a momentary hint of approval. It was fleeting.

'I just hope you're right, Sister. But as we have no choice, let's get to it.'

She was already signalling to Nurse Forbes and within minutes the trolley was ready and the vital blood sample off to the lab. Clearing away she purposely avoided looking at Tim, knowing that if she spoke now she would say something she would regret. As if he seemed to sense it, he took one look

at her grim face, turned on his heel and left the
ward.

She had almost forgotten Oliver Steele's presence until he handed her the last of the case notes
and subjected her pale face to a long, cool scrutiny.
Somehow it seemed to stretch her taut nerves even
more and she had to battle hard against a sudden
urge to burst into tears. None of which, she was
sure, escaped him for one moment.

'I don't like having to disagree with Mr Sinclair,
Sister, but I would say that you are by no means fit
to be back on duty. I suggest that you take at least a
couple of days off, and the sooner the better.'

Tight-lipped, she turned away, making a pretence of checking the trolley. 'I'm perfectly all
right, sir. Just a little tired, that's all.'

'You may think so, Sister.' A brief flash of irritation crossed his face. 'The point is that I don't care
to have emotionally overwrought nurses on my
ward. They are of little use either to me or to the
patients.'

She turned to face him, her face white with
anger. 'I believe I am perfectly capable of doing
my job properly, sir.' Her hands shook and she
clenched them purposely together, wishing the
thumping in her head would stop. 'I can only
apologise for what happened over Mr Lumley's
blood tests. They should have been done and it was
my responsibility to see to it that they were . . .'

'I think you are purposely misunderstanding me,
Sara.' His voice was very quiet. 'In any case, the
responsibility was not yours, it was Lawson's. He

and I, and I'm sure you, are fully aware of that fact and whilst your sense of loyalty is admirable, Sara, I warn you it is also sadly misplaced.'

She stared at him, not even knowing what had made her try to protect Tim. There was no excusing what he had done, or rather, omitted to do. Perhaps, as Oliver Steele had said, it was a misguided sense of loyalty, but what hurt most was that this man should have misinterpreted her motives. It wasn't because she loved Tim. But how could she tell him that, when it would also mean confessing that she suddenly realised that the only man who could ever mean anything in her life was standing in front of her now, dark hair falling over his forehead, a worried look on his face, and totally indifferent to the fact that she loved him.

CHAPTER ELEVEN

IT WAS a relief to get to the end of the week and know that she had a whole weekend off. It was a completely last minute decision to go home, but somehow all her previous plans of washing her clothes and restoring the contents of her wardrobe to some sort of order before winter set in with a vengeance, suddenly lost their attractions, even if she had had the energy, which she didn't.

It was odd that it seemed to be taking such a long time to get over the accident, she thought. Physically there was absolutely no reason why she shouldn't be back to normal, yet mentally she felt tired and depressed, as if everything was too much of an effort. What she needed was to get away, relax completely, with time to try and get things into perspective. It seemed to be becoming a habit lately, she thought, as she threw a few clothes into a suitcase and tossed it into the back of the car.

The rain actually gave way to sunshine as she drove the last few miles along lanes where the hedges and trees were rapidly beginning to change colour. It came through the car windows, striking warmly against her face and arms, and for the first time in days she began to relax, as if her whole body was gradually being freed from tension. Not that there was any point in fooling herself that anything could be solved simply by escaping for a few days. It would still all be there, waiting for her when she got back . . . unless of course she didn't go back.

The idea hit her with such force that, for a moment, her attention was distracted from the road, and she had to fight to bring her concentration back. Leaving Clem's? It was something she would dread doing, yet what was the alternative? To stay and work with Oliver Steele, as if nothing had happened? Under the circumstances, that didn't seem possible, not when even the mere sight of him was enough to throw her normally well controlled emotions into conflict.

She forced herself to put Oliver Steele out of her mind as she turned the car into the drive and came to a halt at the foot of the steps. A whole weekend stretched ahead and she wasn't going to spend it worrying over precisely those things she was hoping to escape.

Unloading her suitcase from the car she stood for a moment, letting her gaze take in the familiar order of the gardens which were her father's pride and joy. The roses were still beautiful and large pots of plants trailed in flashes of brilliant colour from the terrace. She had often thought that if her father hadn't made medicine his life's work he would have been content to work with the soil, watching things grow, creating life. But perhaps it was all part of the same pattern, she mused, and noticed for the first time that the lawns needed cutting and the edges neatening. It was unusual to see even so small a sign of neglect and a twinge of alarm ran through her, a feeling which was pushed hastily aside as Mrs Meakin came down the steps towards her, her face lighting with pleasure.

'Miss Sara, how nice! Why didn't you let us know you were coming? I could have made something special for dinner.'

'I didn't know myself, Milly, until the last minute.' Sara picked her bag up from the front seat and closed the car door. 'It was strictly a spur of the moment decision.' She glanced up at the house. 'Oh lor, Daddy doesn't have guests for the weekend, does he? I didn't even think.'

'Bless you, no. He doesn't entertain so much these days.' Milly insisted on taking a small bag. 'He did mention vaguely that someone may pay a brief call but I don't think it's definite. In any case you know it wouldn't make any difference. Your room is always kept ready. The professor insists on it, you know that.'

Sara smiled and didn't add that her reasons had been purely selfish, because she needed to be quiet and had come away purposely to avoid company. 'Yes, of course. How is my father anyway?' She saw the swift frown of concern which briefly clouded the woman's features.

'Well I can't say I'm not worried and that's the truth. In fact that's one reason I'm so pleased to see you. Not that I'm not always of course, but I've thought the professor seemed very tired lately and he's taken to resting more, which isn't like him at all. You know how stubborn he is as a rule.'

By now Sara's steps had quickened as she walked

into the house. 'Yes, I do indeed. Where is he, Milly? If he's resting now I won't disturb him.'

'No, I don't think so. I left him in the library reading, although he may well be having a doze. He seems to like to take a nap now in the afternoons. Not that I'm supposed to notice, of course.'

Leaving her case in the hall, Sara made her way towards the library and opened the door quietly. She didn't know quite what she had expected but the man sleeping in the chair, his head resting back, the face, even in sleep, drawn with pain, seemed to bear so little resemblance to the father she knew that for an instant it was almost as if her heart stopped beating.

She moved slowly towards him and as she did so his eyelids flickered and opened. Like the rest of him they seemed tissue-paper thin and his lips had the blueish tinge she had dreaded to see.

'Sara, my dear, what a lovely surprise! Why didn't you tell me? I was just reading through some papers and must have missed hearing your car or I would have come to meet you.'

She went along with the pretence as she bent to kiss him, painfully conscious that he seemed to be fighting for breath, much as he tried to hide it. 'I thought I'd surprise you. Anyway, I guessed you'd be working and I didn't want to disturb you. Look I'll tell you what, I'll take my things up to my room and have a shower, then I'll come and chat to you later, shall I? We can have tea together if you like when I've washed away some of the dust.'

It was the best excuse she could think of to give

him time to recover, and she knew that he would be grateful for it. She was right. When she came downstairs an hour later he was more like his old self but moving, she noticed, much more slowly than she remembered, and he seemed to be exhausted by the slightest movement.

Pouring tea she passed him a cup and sandwiches and they sat chatting.

'You're looking tired, Sara. Are they working you too hard at that hospital?'

She smiled. 'You always say that.'

'Perhaps because it's true, only this time it's something more, isn't it?'

She toyed with a sandwich, purposely answering lightly, 'Not really.' It was all too complicated to explain, even if she had known how to begin. 'We've just been extra busy, that's all. Short of staff, rushed off our feet. You know how it is? That's why I thought it would do me good to get away for a while.' She put her cup down and stretched lazily. 'The flat is very nice and convenient but it's still on top of the job somehow, whereas this house is like another world. It's funny, have you ever noticed how you don't even notice the smell of antiseptic until it isn't there?'

He laughed. 'Your mother always used to say I brought it home with me and she was probably right. Some things you can't get rid of, no matter how hard you try.'

The same could be said of feelings, she thought. She smiled and poured more tea, knowing that her father wasn't fooled.

'And where's that young man of yours again? Too busy to come, was he?'

She stirred her tea vigorously. 'Something like that.'

'He's not the right one for you, Sara.'

She swallowed the too-hot tea and got to her feet, carrying the cup with her to the window. 'I thought you liked Tim.'

'And so I did, on the few occasions I met him. I'm sure he's a very nice young man, but I take it things got rather more serious than you intended. Is that it, or am I prying?'

Her mouth twisted, wryly. 'Of course not, and in a way I suppose you're right.'

'I take it he wants to marry you? He'd be a fool if he didn't.'

'Don't you think you may be just very slightly prejudiced?'

'A father's prerogative.' He watched as she brushed a strand of hair from her eyes. 'Are you going to?'

Her shoulders rose. 'I don't think so.'

'But you're not sure?'

She sighed. 'No . . . yes.'

'Well at least that sounds fairly decisive.'

In spite of herself she had to laugh. 'Oh I don't know. It's never that simple, somehow.'

'Things never are.' He was quiet, as if realising that she needed to be alone with her thoughts.

The truth was that it wasn't Tim who was causing her confusion. Yes, she was fond of him, very fond, and probably always would be, in a way. It wasn't easy to banish two years from your life forever, especially when there was nothing to replace them, and it was the thought of the empty years ahead which filled her with such terror, the years and the knowledge that the man she really loved wasn't even aware of her existence, except as a source of constant irritation. None of which, she sighed, was a good enough reason to marry Tim.

She was right. It was good to be home. After only a few hours she felt the tensions beginning to slip away. She had slept like a log and got up early to go for a long, brisk walk. Her father was still sleeping and she was careful not to disturb him as she let herself out of the house and set off down the lane to walk through the nearby woods.

She was wearing a warm jacket over a skirt and jumper and had actually remembered to bring a pair of boots with her. She was glad she had them now as the early morning chill hit her, bringing a glow to her cheeks and ruffling her hair which she had purposely brushed and left loose.

It was a beautiful morning with the first hint of autumn in the air and mist clinging to the fields and hedgerows. If only she didn't have to leave it all behind. A weekend was too short a time but it was all she had and somehow, before she returned to Clem's she must try to find an answer. Either that or learn to live with things the way they were, and there seemed little chance of doing that.

It was mid-morning before she returned to the house to find that her father had stayed in bed late.

'But he'll be up for lunch,' Milly told her. She was bustling round the kitchen as Sara came in, took off her jacket and sat at the table.

'It isn't like him, is it?' She drank coffee and ate home-made scones with butter.

'No it isn't. I thought he was looking a bit peaky when I took him a cup of tea but when I suggested calling the doctor he wouldn't hear of it. You know how he is. Said he was perfectly capable of getting up as usual, which he is doing.' Milly pursed her lips and put the empty crockery noisily into the sink. However, when the professor finally emerged, Sara was pleased to see him looking relatively bright and he ate a reasonable lunch.

'I wonder if you'd mind taking some letters to the post office in town for me,' he asked as they finished their coffee after the meal. 'They're rather important. I promised to send a series of papers over to Professor Thomas. You know, he went to Canada last year. I think he'll find them quite useful in some new surgery technique he's trying out.'

'Yes of course I will, I'll go as soon as I've finished. In fact I'll be glad of the exercise. Walking the wards all day isn't quite the same somehow.'

'I'd take them myself but there are one or two things I have to sort out here and some work I want to finish.'

'You'll remember this is Saturday, won't you, and not work too hard?'

'My dear Sara, I never work too hard, and since when did one day differ from the rest?' But he smiled, pressing her hand reassuringly. 'Go on, and don't feel you need to hurry back. I shall be perfectly all right. You enjoy your freedom while you have the chance.'

'Well if you're sure. As it happens, I would rather like to look for a new dress while I'm out.' She had been promising herself for some time that she would find something to wear which offered a sharp contrast to the plainness of the uniform she wore every day. Not that she disliked it, on the contrary, but there were times, increasingly more lately, when she felt that her life was in danger of being taken over by the hospital and by the people in it.

She drove into town, posted the letters and spent a pleasant hour re-aquainting herself with the local shops. She treated herself not only to the luxury of a new dress in a shade of russet which particularly suited her, but also to a very pretty blouse, and she even managed to find a book in the local second-hand shop which her father had been looking for for ages.

Well satisfied with her purchases, she drove back feeling her good humour almost entirely restored. Unfortunately it was banished the instant she entered the drive and her gaze came to rest on the large, black car which was parked there. At once her heart began a crazy little dance.

'Oh no, it couldn't be.' Perhaps there was some mistake. There had to be more than one car like that in this part of the world. Oliver Steele didn't have the monopoly . . . or did he?

But even as she entered the house and made her

way to the library she knew she was wrong. The face which turned to look so appraisingly in her direction as she walked into the room, her cheeks flushed, her hair wind-blown, was definitely none other than that of the senior consultant.

CHAPTER TWELVE

'AH, SARA, my dear, come and meet my guest. But of course you know each other already, don't you.'

She knew that she was staring and even as her own cold hand was clasped within Oliver Steele's warm one, she felt the angry resentment welling up. What right had he to be here? She had worked so hard simply to banish him from her thoughts and yet here he was, calmly striding into her life again in the one place where she had thought she was bound to be safe.

'Yes, I think we know each other very well, don't we, Sister?' He was looking directly at her as he spoke, making no attempt to release her hand and, as if sensing the thoughts behind her angry green eyes, said softly, 'When your father invited me I had no idea you would be here. I somehow imagined you would be . . . otherwise engaged.'

Implying, she thought, that if he had known he certainly wouldn't have come. Well that wasn't going to cause any problems. This was her home, she had planned a quiet weekend and that was what she intended to have. 'I do like to get away occasionally,' she muttered coldly, detaching her hand from his grasp. 'And you yourself suggested it, if you remember?'

Clutching defensively at her parcels she calculated that if she kept out of the way for a couple of hours he would have left by the time she came back. 'Well, it was nice to see you, Sir.' She smiled sweetly and headed for the door, but it was her father who unwittingly shattered the illusion.

'Oh come on now, surely we can skip the formality. You're not on duty now, either of you. Sara, this is Oliver. Oliver, this is Sara, and how about some coffee, my dear, if you wouldn't mind asking Milly.'

She thought she detected just the faintest trace of amusement in Oliver Steele's eyes as she gritted her teeth and marched out of the door. Minutes later she returned, carrying the tray herself because Milly had just been about to take a batch of cakes from the oven.

She put the tray on to the coffee table in time to hear her father say, 'But of course you must stay to dinner. Mrs Meakin doesn't mind, in fact I'd already warned her there would be a guest. Besides, it will be company for Sara. I'm afraid I haven't exactly been good company for her.'

'Nonsense,' she said stiffly as she handed him his coffee, purposely avoiding looking in Oliver Steele's direction. Her father was looking very tired again. 'I came here to relax. I just wish you would do the same. By the way, I managed to find one of those books you've been looking for.'

'That's marvellous. I don't get the chance to go into town as often as I'd like these days.'

'I'll bring it down for you later, as long as you promise not to sit up all night reading it.'

She moved back to the tray, blushing faintly as she became conscious of Oliver Steele's gaze fixed upon her. He took the cup from her and she couldn't help noticing the slight tension around his mouth though it vanished as her father began speaking again. Soon the two of them were so involved in some medical discussion that she knew they scarcely even noticed when she muttered some excuse and slipped quietly out of the room.

The telephone began to ring just as she reached the hall. For a moment she was almost tempted to ignore it, then knew that she couldn't. It scarcely came as a surprise to hear Tim's voice sounding vaguely hurt and accusing at the other end of the line.

'Hello, Sara. For heaven's sake, why didn't you say you were going away for the weekend? I felt like an idiot looking everywhere for you and having to be told by some nurse that you'd decided to go home.'

'Well it was rather a spur of the moment decision,' she said, wondering with a vague sense of irritation why she should sound so apologetic.

There was a slight pause. 'If you'd told me I would have come with you. I could have arranged to swop duties somehow. I'm off tomorrow anyway.'

'No . . . I . . . I'm sorry, Tim, I didn't really think about it. In any case I wanted to be alone for a while. You do understand, don't you?'

She could almost sense him frowning at the other end of the phone. 'Well, no, as a matter of fact I can't honestly say I do. It isn't like you, Sara, just going off like that.'

No, she didn't suppose it was. 'I did say I'm sorry,' she repeated, instilling a note of firmness into her voice.

'I don't understand. You're sure you're all right? I mean, you are over the accident properly?'.

'Yes of course I am. I promise you there was nothing even slightly sinister in my motives for disappearing. I was just tired and felt like getting away from it all for a while, that's all.'

'Away from me, Sara?'

She bit back a sigh, her hand tightening on the receiver. 'I didn't say that, Tim. Don't put words into my mouth.'

'But that's precisely what I'd like to do. You know you promised to think things over, well I want you to say "yes". You are still thinking about it, aren't you, darling?'

From the corner of her eye she suddenly realised that the library door was open and that Oliver Steele was standing watching her. She wondered how much he had heard and decided that it scarcely made any difference anyway. Even so she felt inhibited by his presence and, without being aware of it, her voice shook as she said, 'Yes, I am still thinking about it, Tim, I promise.'

'And you'll give me your answer soon?'

She could hear the relief in his voice as she said she would. Putting the phone down, she wondered why she hadn't simply been honest with Tim and told him there was no possibility of her marrying him. Her brain just didn't seem to be functioning properly. She felt tired, flustered and under pressure, and the presence of the man beside her didn't help.

'Sorry to intrude.' There was a note of mockery in his voice. 'I just came out to say that if it's going to cause any inconvenience I can always make my excuses and get away before dinner tonight.'

She had to fight the temptation to take him at his word. 'There's no need for that. You're my father's guest and it does him good to have someone to talk to.' She turned away but his hand detained her, resting on her arm.

'But you would rather I didn't stay, wouldn't you, Sara?'

She stared at him. Was that what she wanted? His nearness only seemed to add complications to her life. She shook her head. 'It really doesn't matter to me one way or the other.'

'Are you so sure?'

Without even giving her a chance to answer, suddenly he was leading her out into the garden, ignoring her protests that her father would miss them.

'The professor is perfectly all right, I assure you. I left him studying some reports I brought with me.'

'Is it really necessary to work him so hard?' Her eyes flashed angrily. 'Can't you see he's a sick man, that I worry about him?' Before she realised it the tears were coursing down her cheeks and with one gruff oath he had taken her in his arms and was smoothing back her hair as he kissed her gently.

'Don't, Sara, don't, my love. This isn't what he would want. You told me that yourself, remember?'

She felt incapable of remembering anything except that she was in his arms and that it seemed right, as if her place had always been there and she didn't want him to let her go again. They clung together, her body offering no resistance against the urgency she sensed in him now. His mouth became ruthless, creating a desire in her so great that she moaned softly, hardly recognising the sound as coming from herself.

'Sara.' His voice was husky with a need which she knew, unashamedly, equalled her own. Whether what he felt was love she had no way of knowing and didn't care as the lean face and dark eyes moved closer again, drawing her relentlessly back into the whirlpool. Nothing seemed important beyond the fact that he was here, now, and that the feelings which were consuming her were like nothing she had ever known with Tim.

Whether it was that brief unbidden memory which caused her to stiffen in his arms, or that she had been subconsciously aware of Milly's high-pitched voice calling her from a distance as she ran down the steps towards them, she never knew. She only knew that one minute she was in his arms and in the next her world seemed to shatter almost as if she had had a premonition.

'Miss Sara, Miss Sara, come quickly. It's the professor.'

There was blind panic in the voice. Sara knew

that Oliver Steele was beside her as she turned and even as she began to run blindly towards the house his hand was beneath her arm, preventing her from stumbling, as if he had sensed that without it she would have fallen.

His face was grim as he reached the library ahead of her. He was beside the crumpled figure of her father before she could reach him and was quickly but deftly removing the man's tie, feeling for a pulse, then tearing open the shabby old jacket. Soon his fist was thudding down upon a heart which had ceased, very quietly, very gently, to beat.

She heard herself sobbing quietly, 'Oh no, no, not like this,' before Oliver's voice penetrated sharply into her brain.

'Call an ambulance, Sara. Cardiac arrest.' And then, as she stood frozen. 'For God's sake, move.'

She did move, though everything seemed to be happening in slow motion. Her breath was stuck in her lungs, needing a desperate effort to drive it upwards. Her fingers dialled the number. She heard her own voice sounding strangely calm and wondered how it was possible when her whole brain was in turmoil, refusing to accept what was happening even though she had seen it with her own eyes. Her father lying crumpled on the floor, his face crumpled in a spasm of pain . . . She had seen it all before, but then it had been someone else. It was only now that she realised the full intensity of the horror people felt when it was one of their own loved ones stricken down.

Milly was sobbing quietly in the doorway, apron

pressed to her mouth as Sara knelt beside Oliver. His own actions and softly spoken words brought her back to reality and she found herself moving instinctively, her actions becoming automatic.

'I have a heart beat. It's faint, but there. We just have to keep it going. Where the hell is that ambulance?' He cast a quick glance over his shoulder at her stricken face. 'He's still alive, Sara. Bear up, he needs you now.'

She nodded, her throat so tight that speech hurt. 'I'm going with him.'

He didn't argue. 'I'll take you in my car.'

'But you don't . . .'

'There's no way I'm going to leave you, Sara.'

He couldn't have said anything she wanted to hear more. It was his nearness which kept her going as the ambulance arrived and her father was carried out wrapped in blankets and gently lifted inside to one of the beds.

As the doors closed, shutting him out of sight, she shivered and Oliver's arm tightened round her. 'Come on, we'll get there as he arrives. Just don't give up hope. He's still alive, that's what matters.'

Oliver was still there as they walked beside the trolley, along seemingly endless corridors. Doctors arrived, familiar figures, but she scarcely noticed. She had eyes only for the man on the trolley as he was whisked into the special coronary unit and again doors closed, quietly excluding her.

'Let them do what they have to do,' Oliver advised, leading her gently to one of the chairs, still holding her. 'They'll let you see him as soon as possible. For now it's best we keep out of the way.'

He brought her coffee. It was hot, too hot, but she swallowed it, watching the doors, trembling at every sound.

When the white-coated figure came out she needed only one look at his face to tell her that it was over. Strangely she didn't feel able to cry just then. It had all happened too quickly. But perhaps that was best. Her father wasn't the kind of man who would have wanted anything less than a life in which he could be fully active.

People came out of the room slowly, glancing in her direction before they hurried away, some offering condolences. It didn't mean anything, not even when they said she could see her father. It might have been a stranger lying there. For some reason she thought of the book she had given him and which he would never read.

'Come on, I'm taking you home. There's nothing more you can do.'

As Oliver drove her back to the house she felt herself becoming strangely calmer. It was almost as if, in accepting that her father was gone, it became easier to bear.

'I'll let them know at the hospital that you won't be in. You'll want some time to arrange things.'

She nodded. 'It's strange. I keep thinking I should feel . . . more, and yet all I really feel is relief that he didn't suffer and most of all that he didn't recover only to live a half-life. He would have hated that more than anything.'

His gaze shifted briefly from the road to her face. 'He was a fine man. A lot of people will remember him and the things he did with a great deal of admiration, affection and gratitude. But what about you, Sara, what are you going to do now?'

She looked at him then away again to stare out of the window. 'I don't know. Somehow it doesn't seem important right now.' She didn't even realise that the tears were streaming down her face.

It was dark by the time they reached the house. She half expected him to leave her but he didn't. He took the key from her lifeless fingers and opened the door. 'I'm going to fix you a good strong drink.'

Gratitude flooded through her, mixed with relief. She couldn't have borne to be alone right now, especially not in this room where everything was still as they had left it.

A sob caught in her throat as she stared at him bleakly, then before she knew what was happening he was kissing her urgently, the pressure of his mouth hard against hers. When he released her briefly, she murmured, 'Don't go, don't leave me.'

'Don't worry, Sara, I don't intend to, ever again.'

She knew then that she wanted him to stay. Her head rested against his shoulder. He moved to raise her chin and kiss her again, murmuring her name softly. She responded unashamedly and was drawn closer against the strong, hard masculinity of him, her lips parting eagerly and feeling the same hungry response in him.

'I love you, Sara.' His voice was hoarse before his

mouth claimed hers yet again and she felt herself lifted and carried to the sofa. His name escaped from her lips and he groaned softly as he looked briefly but searchingly into her eyes and read the message there. She could feel his heart thudding as he gathered her close, brushing back her hair and seeking her mouth. 'I've waited so long, Sara. I want you, you know that, but I also want you to be sure.'

She was sure. More sure than she had ever been of anything in her life. The emotions she was experiencing now were like none she had ever known with Tim, and she realised now that they never could be. Ironically, the mere thought of Tim made her stiffen just for a second in his arms and he frowned, staring down at her, as if sensing her sudden hesitation.

'What is it, Sara? What's wrong?'

She wanted to tell him that it was nothing. To explain that suddenly she knew very clearly that Tim meant nothing to her and everything was going to be all right. Then the telephone rang and she flinched involuntarily, feeling him draw away from her, frowning, puzzled.

'I'm sorry, Sara.' His face was taut and she knew from the stricken look in his eyes that he had totally misinterpreted her brief hesitation.

'You don't understand.' She flung out a hand appealingly and in desperation reached out to silence the phone.

Tim's voice sounded breathless, awkward. 'Hello, Sara, darling. I've only just got back to the hospital and heard the news. My God, I'm so sorry . . .'

'Tim.' Her voice seemed to be trapped in her throat as Oliver looked at her and slowly began to move towards the door. 'It's all right, Sara,' he said quietly. 'I understand perfectly. I won't bother you again.'

He was gone before she could say a word. She stared bleakly at the door, scarcely hearing anything as Tim's voice continued to speak in her ear.

CHAPTER THIRTEEN

'OF COURSE you must take as much time as you need.' Miss Baxter's voice was quietly reassuring. 'Staff nurse is coping beautifully and sister covers when necessary so you mustn't worry on that score.'

Sara sat, hands clasped neatly out of habit in her lap as she looked at the DNS. It seemed strange to be sitting here wearing outdoor clothes rather than uniform.

'I'm very grateful. I hate letting you down. It's just that everything happened so quickly.'

'My dear girl, there's no question of letting us down. I can imagine what a shock it must have been for you.' Miss Baxter frowned, her attractive face full of sympathy. 'The professor is going to be sadly missed. He was very popular with all members of staff.'

Sara nodded, still experiencing the strange feeling that they were talking about someone else.

'Would you like me to arrange for you to take some annual leave? I'm sure we could cover you for a week, maybe longer.'

Sara shook her head quickly. What she needed now more than anything was to get back to work, to keep her mind off things. Perhaps she was still in a state of shock. The funeral was something she had lived through as if it were a dream. The church had been filled to overflowing with friends and colleagues of her father. She had even caught a brief glimpse of Oliver, standing tight-lipped at the back of the church, and her heart had leaped crazily with joy for a second or two. But later, when she had had a chance to look for him to try to explain, he had already vanished.

She dragged herself back to the woman who was speaking. 'No, I'd really rather not.' She answered the query. 'To be honest I feel the less time I have to brood the better.'

'Yes, I'm sure you're wise.'

'I have to see the solicitor of course. But I'm sure everything will be quite straightforward. Then I must do some sorting out.' Her chin rose and she resisted the urge to probe at the dull ache in her temple. 'But I shall be back on duty in a couple of days if that's all right?'

'Yes, of course, Sister. If there is anything at all we can do to help . . .'

Sara turned to stare out of the window and wondered what anyone could do to put her shattered life together again. She uttered a deep sigh, drew in a breath and turned to look at the woman sitting opposite. 'As a matter of fact . . . I've decided to hand in my notice.' The words were out even before she had time to think. She registered the look of shock in Miss Baxter's eyes and found it vaguely gratifying to know that in some respects at least she would be missed, if only in a professional capacity.

'But why?' The inevitable questions came and Sara wasn't even sure that she had the answers, or at least none that seemed right. It was all too confusing, too impossible to explain that she couldn't go on working in the same hospital with the man she loved and who didn't even acknowledge her existence.

'Yes, I've been very happy here.' She heard herself say dully. But that was when she had imagined her life revolved around Tim. It was odd now to realise just how narrow her horizons had been, that somehow she might have been content to let herself drift along and, in time, perhaps even into marriage, if Oliver Steele hadn't come along and turned her life, her whole existence upside down.

'I just feel I need a change, to get away for a while.'

Miss Baxter was staring at her, totally uncomprehending. 'I can't help feeling you're behaving a little rashly, Sister. Of course I realise your father's death came as a considerable shock . . .'

Sara listened without really hearing. 'It isn't just that.' It was too many things. Tim's sudden departure for Canada had been part of it. She had seen it coming of course but the speed of it had shaken her complacency badly somehow, coming on top of everything else. Her thoughts went back to their last meeting when she had told him quite calmly that she didn't love him and couldn't marry him. She had waited for the arguments and protestations, but they had never come. In fact the calmness with which he had accepted it had shaken her—he had looked at her for a long moment then shrugged and said simply, 'Well I can't say it comes as any surprise. It wouldn't have worked out anyway, would it Sara? I suppose it's Steele, isn't it?'

She had denied it even as she registered the fact that all she had thought she and Tim had together had been dismissed with a kind of negligence which hurt. Had it really meant so little to him?

'No, there's no one else, Tim.' It hadn't been a lie. She hadn't seen or heard a single word from Oliver since that night, and if he was purposely avoiding her then he was succeeding admirably. He even contrived to make his rounds these days when he must know she was most likely to be absent from the ward.

The next thing she heard was that Tim had handed in his notice, sold his car and flown out to Canada.

The more she thought about it, the more a fresh start seemed the only answer. Perhaps away from Clem's, without constant reminders, she might eventually, if not entirely, forget Oliver Steele, manage to think about him without that awful, icy ache in her heart.

She looked directly at Miss Baxter. 'I've given it a great deal of thought and I'd like to leave at the end of the month if that won't cause too much inconvenience.'

Miss Baxter's finely traced brows winged together in an expression of extreme disappointment. 'Well all I can say is that I'm very sorry,

Sister. You'll be a great loss to us. Perhaps if you change your mind you'll come and see me again.'

But as she walked out of the office, Sara knew there was no chance of that, not as long as Oliver Steele was around.

She had driven to the solicitors' where, as she had expected, everything had been perfectly straightforward. Even so, by mid-afternoon when she finally got back to the house she was feeling drained both physically and mentally. She made a firm decision to put off the business of sorting out papers and generally discovering what needed to be done. There was her own life to be considered, and what she was going to do with that. But she felt no regrets for the suddenness of her decision to hand in her notice, even though it meant that in a few weeks she was going to be without a job.

She found Milly in the kitchen, red-eyed and kneading bread dough with a far greater effort than it warranted, but she looked up, wiping her hands as Sara sat wearily at the well worn oak table.

'Let's have coffee, Milly. I'm sure we could both do with it.'

'The kettle's hot. Shall I bring it through to the library?'

'No, here will be fine.' Sara didn't want to admit that even now she kept expecting to see her father sitting in his favourite chair. 'Besides, we can talk.'

She caught the quick look of relief on Milly's face and knew she must have been wondering what was going to happen. Well, in that respect at least she could put her mind at rest, and proceeded to do so.

'I've been hoping you'll stay on, Milly, if you'd like to, that is. Someone will obviously have to look after the house and it would be too much for me with my work.'

The woman's expression told her clearly enough that it was precisely what she had been hoping for. 'I've been wondering what I'd do. I've been here for so long, looking after the professor and your mother, bless her. I just couldn't imagine anything else somehow. But what about your nice little flat? Won't a house like this be too big for you on your own? It was all right for the professor, but he used to entertain occasionally.'

It was something Sara had been thinking about too. The flat had been so convenient, only a short distance from Clem's. But if she was going to leave the hospital that wouldn't matter any more. She felt a momentary sensation of panic and cupped her hands round the coffee mug.

'I don't really have things straight in my own mind yet, Milly, but I do know that I shall always want this house to be here.' She got up and carried her coffee to the window, thinking that even the house wouldn't be the same ever again because every time she thought of it, she would think of Oliver and the gardens. Without turning she said, 'I've decided to look for a job somewhere else, Milly. I think I need a change.' She knew the woman was staring at her.

'Leave St Clement's? But you love it there.' Emotions flickered across her face. 'It's not because of that young man of yours, is it, him upping and going off to Canada like that?'

Sara managed a smile. 'No, it's not because of Tim, Milly, at least not directly. I just need to get away, that's all. As a matter of fact I've applied for a post in Exeter.' She had seen the advertisement and had written her application before even giving herself time to think about it. 'I've been asked to go for interview but nothing is definite. I don't suppose I'll get it though. The competition is bound to be pretty fierce.'

'Oh of course you'll get it. You're good at your job,' Milly insisted loyally.

Sara smiled. 'Anyway, I don't want you to worry about *your* job. I spoke to the solicitor and Daddy made ample provision for you to stay as long as you like, so it's up to you. The solicitor will be writing to you to let you know the details. I'd like you to stay, you know that.'

Milly blew her nose hard. 'Well yes, of course I will. Bless you, where else would I go?' Her face lifted stubbornly. 'I'll stay as long as the house is yours. If you decide to sell, well then that's another matter. But I must say it would be a shame, a lovely house like this. It ought to be lived in by a family. Someone who would appreciate it.'

Sara poured herself another cup of coffee, trying to swallow the sudden tightness in her throat. Milly was right, the house did need a family, but it didn't look as if it was ever going to be her own which filled the rooms and the lovely garden.

*   *   *

She made an early start next morning, telling herself that the sorting out had to be done and the sooner she got it over with the better, especially as she fully intended returning to the hospital the next day. It was a decision she had come to in the early hours of the morning. She knew she could easily have taken more time off, but what she needed was to be kept busy and she would certainly be that on Men's Surgical.

She knew from the single glance she had stolen in the mirror that she looked pale and drained. Her eyes were dark ringed and she hadn't even bothered to apply the light covering of make-up she usually wore when she went on duty. After all, no one would see so it didn't matter. She had dressed in a pair of old jeans and a shirt and had left her hair loose. The fact that it made her look about sixteen years old and ridiculously vulnerable didn't occur to her because she hadn't cast more than a casual disinterested glance at her image in the mirror. They simply seemed the most sensible things to wear for the task in hand and she realised, as she sat on the floor, surrounded by a mass of old books and papers, a smut of dust on her nose, that she had been right.

It was a thankless task. Most of the things she knew she could never part with, except for letters which were faded and torn and which her father had probably kept because he was a hoarder. By the end of the morning as she reviewed several hours of work and the one small but full wastepaper basket which had resulted from it, she knew she was going to have to be more ruthless.

After a light meal which Milly brought in on a tray and which she ate without even caring what it was, she began again, this time trying to be more positive. But it was no use. Tears sprang to her eyes and she sat on the floor, her face buried in her hands. Somehow she was going to have to do it. Things had to be put in order before she started her new job, but it was too soon. There were too many painful reminders.

It was only as the doorbell rang and continued to ring that she remembered Milly saying something about going into town to do some shopping and, with a sigh of exasperation she brushed a hand across her eyes and went to the door.

At the sight of the tall figure standing there her face paled and then flushed. 'Oliver . . . Sir . . .' She didn't know whether to laugh or cry. As she stared at him, her eyes noted only the grim set of his jaw and the fact that he looked very tired. She resented the sudden feeling of vulnerability his presence seemed to cause.

'I have to talk to you, Sara.'

Her chin rose. It was cruel of him to come here now, like this. 'I really don't think we have anything to say to one another and I'm very busy, if you wouldn't mind . . .'

She attempted to close the door, only to gasp as he ignored her protest and stepped inside. His face was unsmiling as he said, 'As it happens, I do mind, Sara, very much. I don't intend leaving until I've said what I came to say.'

She hesitated, then stepped aside grudgingly. He was wearing a dark suit and she caught the subtle smell of his after-shave as he brushed past her. 'Well, as long as it won't take too long. I have a great deal to do.'

He didn't even seem to be listening as he strode into the library and waited for her to join him. She did so warily, shifting a pile of books from a chair, but he made no attempt to sit down. Instead he glowered at her, making her feel very small, and she wished she hadn't told Milly she could take the afternoon off.

'I really am busy,' she said defensively, and saw the nerve in his jaw tense as he looked at her. His gaze took in the disorder of the room then flicked back to her flushed cheeks.

'Would you like coffee?' She had moved instinctively towards the door as she said it, but to her chagrin, he managed somehow to place himself between it and her, thus neatly cutting off her escape as if he had suspected what she had in mind.

'No, I don't want coffee, Sara. Nor do I intend playing games.' He gazed at the piles of books she had sorted which were stacked at random on the desk. 'So it's true, you are leaving.'

Her heart missed a beat. The grapevine was obviously in good order and no doubt making the most of the situation. Her last conversation with Jane had confirmed that several of the nurses believed she was going out to join Tim in Canada, but she hadn't felt inclined to disillusion them. What did it matter anyway? Her chin rose as she said quietly, 'I really don't see that it's any concern of yours, but yes, I gave a month's notice which Miss Baxter accepted.'

For a moment he stared at her in grim silence then he said scathingly, 'And just what do you hope to gain by running away?'

She couldn't help gasping. 'Running away? I don't know what you mean, and in any case, what I do with my private life is no concern of yours.'

'Isn't it, Sara?' Suddenly he was menacingly close and with the slightest movement his hand caught her wrist just as she was about to turn away. She struggled but his hold merely tightened and there was something in his expression which made her tremble. 'You crazy little fool! Why give up everything, your career, everything that means anything to you, just for him? He isn't worth it. Can't you see that?'

She stared at him, anger and confusion mingling. He had no idea what meant everything to her. How dare he try to tell her what to do with her life! Hadn't he already caused enough havoc?

'You have no right to tell me what I should or shouldn't do . . .'

'Well, that's a pity,' he said quietly, 'because I'm going to, even though I know it won't make the slightest difference.' He was holding her so tightly, so closely that she could feel the warmth of his breath on her cheek. For an instant she wanted to brush the hair from his eyes, but there was a coldness in his expression which prevented it. 'I suppose you're going to be married out there, is that it?' His face was tense as he said it and she flinched. 'He's no good for you, Sara. Don't you see that?'

Her breath caught in her throat as she tried to free herself from his grasp. His words scarcely made sense but she was too angry, too confused by his nearness to think straight.

'And I suppose you think you know what *is* good for me?'

'As a matter of fact, yes I do.' And before she could speak his mouth had come down brutally on hers in a kiss which bruised her lips, yet which made her senses reel by its sheer sensuality. He was completely ruthless, sparing her nothing as he stripped every vestige of resistance from her. It was totally calculated and it was useless to fight, she knew it even as she tried, only to find her struggles subdued as he relentlessly drew her closer. His hands moved over her body, caressing, tantalising, until she sobbed and clung to him unashamedly. She loved him, that was all there was to it. It was crazy. He had brought her nothing but heartache and yet there would never be anyone else, and her hands rose to draw him closer and return his kiss.

He released her then, so abruptly that she almost fell, would have fallen but for the hand which still held her as he stared at her stricken face. He was breathing hard, his eyes glistening with anger. 'Oh yes, I think I know exactly what is good for you, Sara, and I've no intention of letting you throw your life away by running after that no-good . . .'

She drew in a breath and said shakily, 'I don't know what you're talking about.'

For a moment his gaze narrowed. 'Oh I think you do. You're trying to run away from me now. You're becoming good at it.'

It wasn't true. It was the sheer physical presence of him which was unnerving her, making her legs turn to jelly.

'Will you let me go?' She tried to prise his fingers loose but he held her.

'Not until I've at least had my say.' His face was taut as he stared down at her and she flinched before the contempt she saw in his eyes. 'I didn't believe it at first when I heard you were leaving. I didn't think you'd go through with it, not when I . . . not when . . .'

Her head jerked up. 'Not when you what?'

She heard the silent oath. 'For God's sake, Sara, stop playing games with me. I warn you I play rough and I play to win.'

'But I'm not.' She saw the look of bewilderment in his eyes. 'I'm not playing games. I never have, surely you must know that?'

A nerve pulsed in his jaw. 'But . . . I don't understand. You're leaving?'

'Yes, that's right. I've applied for a job in Exeter.'

'Exeter?' She heard the soft catch of his breath. 'But I thought . . . you were going to marry Lawson?'

She shook her head and managed to smile bleakly. 'I've no intention of marrying Tim and probably never had, although I didn't actually realise it myself until fairly recently.'

The look of wonderment in his eyes seemed to pull at her heart and she felt herself drawn shakily towards him.

'You're telling me you're not going to marry him?'

'Is it really so hard to believe?' she asked softly, and for once the senior consultant seemed at a loss for words.

'It's beginning to look as if I've been a damned fool,' he said hoarsely at last as he lifted her face and stared into her eyes.

'It certainly does . . . Sir.' She couldn't resist the malicious attempt at humour and his mouth tightened before he kissed her firmly, as if punishing her. He broke away at last. 'I really thought you were going to marry him. That night when he rang . . .'

'That night when he rang I'd already made up my mind. Before that in fact. I told him I didn't love him but you didn't give me a chance to explain.' Her eyes were bright with unshed tears as she looked at him. 'Tim told me the next day that he was going to Canada. The funny thing was, he didn't even seem upset. I don't mind admitting that it was something of a blow to my pride, but that didn't last long.'

'And just what the hell do you think you did to mine when I was ready and aching to make love to you and suddenly you seemed to draw back? I was convinced I'd made a mistake, that I'd somehow misinterpreted . . .'

Her hand reached up then to smooth the hair from his eyes. 'I wasn't drawing back. Funnily enough I'd just realised that I'd probably been hopelessly in love with you all along. I wanted you to make love to me, and what I'd been feeling for Tim all this time bore no resemblance at all to what I felt for you.' His hand tightened over her fingers. 'That was when the phone rang and you walked out, and for some reason you seem to have been avoiding me ever since.'

'Only because I didn't trust myself to be near you. Any more than I do now. Have you any idea what you do to me?'

She felt the blood pulsing in her veins as he kissed her again. Afterwards, as she rested her head contentedly against his chest she said softly, 'Somehow I think my father would have approved.'

'My darling Sara, of course he did.'

She turned her head to look at him. 'You mean . . . he knew? You discussed it with him? But how?'

'He certainly did know, and he gave us his blessing. He was quite certain I was the right husband for you and I have to agree.'

'Oh, do you indeed? And I suppose I have some say in this?'

'But of course you do, Sara.' She was imprisoned in his arms and didn't feel inclined to make any attempt to escape. 'You simply have to say

"Yes, Oliver, I love you and I'll marry you at once.'"

In fact it was some time before she could say anything at all. Not until he had kissed her soundly and she had recovered her breath sufficiently to murmur, 'Yes, oh yes.'

'Good, then that's settled. I do like a woman who knows her own mind. As long as it happens to coincide with what I want, of course,' he added quietly. But Sara didn't answer.

Mills & Boon

4 Doctor Nurse Romances
FREE

Coping with the daily tragedies and ordeals of a busy hospital, and sharing the satisfaction of a difficult job well done, people find themselves unexpectedly drawn together. Mills & Boon Doctor Nurse Romances capture perfectly the excitement, the intrigue and the emotions of modern medicine, that so often lead to overwhelming and blissful love. By becoming a regular reader of Mills & Boon Doctor Nurse Romances you can enjoy EIGHT superb new titles every two months plus a whole range of special benefits: your very own personal membership card, a free newsletter packed with recipes, competitions, bargain book offers, plus big cash savings.

AND an Introductory FREE GIFT for YOU.
Turn over the page for details.

**Fill in and send this coupon back today
and we'll send you
4 Introductory
Doctor Nurse Romances yours to keep**

FREE

At the same time we will reserve a
subscription to Mills & Boon
Doctor Nurse Romances for you. Every
two months you will receive the latest
8 new titles, delivered direct to your door.
You don't pay extra for delivery. Postage and
packing is always completely Free.
There is no obligation or commitment —
you receive books only for
as long as you want to.

It's easy! Fill in the coupon below and return it to
**MILLS & BOON READER SERVICE, FREEPOST, P.O. BOX 236,
CROYDON, SURREY CR9 9EL.**

Please note: READERS IN SOUTH AFRICA write to
Mills & Boon Ltd., Postbag X3010,
Randburg 2125, S. Africa.

- -

FREE BOOKS CERTIFICATE

**To: Mills & Boon Reader Service, FREEPOST, P.O. Box 236,
Croydon, Surrey CR9 9EL.**

Please send me, free and without obligation, four Dr. Nurse Romances, and reserve a
Reader Service Subscription for me. If I decide to subscribe I shall receive, following my free
parcel of books, eight new Dr. Nurse Romances every two months for £8.00, post and
packing free. If I decide not to subscribe, I shall write to you within 10 days. The free books
are mine to keep in any case. I understand that I may cancel my subscription at any time
simply by writing to you. I am over 18 years of age.
Please write in BLOCK CAPITALS.

Name_____

Address_____

_____

_____Postcode_____

SEND NO MONEY — TAKE NO RISKS

EP1